A Silence
Shared

A Silence Shared

LALLA ROMANO

Translated from the Italian
by Brian Robert Moore

PUSHKIN PRESS

Pushkin Press
Somerset House, Strand
London WC2R 1LA

Copyright © Lalla Romano Estate
Published by arrangement with The Italian Literary Agency

English translation © 2023 Brian Robert Moore
Introduction © 2023 Brian Robert Moore

A Silence Shared was first published as *Tetto Murato* by Einaudi in Turin, 1957

First published by Pushkin Press in 2023

9 8 7 6 5 4 3 2 1

ISBN 13: 978-1-78227-820-7

Designed and typeset by Tetragon, London
Printed and bound by Clays Ltd, Elcograf S.p.A.

www.pushkinpress.com

Silences

An Introduction by Brian Robert Moore

> *"For me, to write has always been to pluck from the dense and complex fabric of life some image, from the noise of the world some note, and surround them in silence."*

LALLA ROMANO

A Silence Shared is a book cut directly from the fabric of the author's life, a journey through memory in which Lalla Romano's own experiences of World War II are relived, and reinterpreted, from the viewpoint of the novel's protagonist, Giulia. In 1943, after her home in Turin was damaged during the Allied bombings, Romano and her young son went to stay with her parents in Cuneo, the town of penetrating silences that is never referred to by name in the novel. Like the character Stefano, Romano's husband, Innocenzo Monti, had to remain in Turin for work, forcing their family to separate. Prior to her return to Cuneo, Romano, who had published her first collection of poetry in 1941, was working as a teacher and frequently exhibiting as a painter, too—between the late 1920s and early 1930s, she had studied at the art school of Felice Casorati, entering into some of the most vibrant, and most committedly antifascist, artistic circles in Italy at the time. But it was in Cuneo that Romano became more directly engaged politically, joining the antifascist Partito d'Azione (Party of Action). It was also in this period that she grew close to the partisan Adolfo Ruata and his wife Eugenia, the real-life Paolo and Ada, who due to Adolfo's poor health took refuge in the countryside near Cuneo towards the end of the war. *Tetto Murato*, the novel's enigmatic original title, refers to the place name of their hideaway: a *tetto*, the standard Italian word for "roof", signifies in local usage a group of farmhouses, while the seemingly fated adjective, *murato*, or "walled in", echoes the characters' isolation and closeness as they shelter from the dangers of the outside world.

With the Nazi-Fascist occupation and the Italian Resistance raging beyond the house's walls, the novel's true subject is the profound understanding and the delicate, at times strained intimacy that develops between these two couples, as Giulia and occasionally Stefano spend time with Paolo and Ada at their refuge throughout the long winter. Just as Giulia feels an undeniable and magnetic connection with the intelligent yet physically vulnerable Paolo (a victim of Fascist torture), she notices similarities in character that draw together the more assured and vital natures of Stefano and Ada. The experience as lived by Giulia becomes an absorbing and subtly subversive exploration of human affinities, of the mysteries of intellectual and physical attraction, phenomena that are often just hinted at in her narration, remaining understated despite their intensity.

Romano rarely strayed from autobiographical subject matter, and the entirety of her published work, with the exception of a few early stories, is narrated in the first person. Forever rejecting the term "memoir" for her books, Romano acknowledged that *A Silence Shared* was the novel in which she most freely distorted the details of her own life: beyond the difference in name, Giulia is younger than Romano was then, and she is not yet a mother. While Romano described these transformations as arising naturally, it seems the divergence between protagonist and author was not taken lightly: in early drafts, the book wasn't told from Giulia's point of view, but from the distanced perspective of a third-person narrator, a conspicuous aspect for a writer who would declare, "I feel I'm in reality, with my feet on the ground, only if I say 'I'." The conscious shift to the first person highlights, perhaps more than any other point in her literary output, Romano's willingness and determination to "say I", an artistic choice from which she would never again waver. In the particular case of *A Silence Shared*, this entails a decision to identify with her protagonist Giulia and to make their reality a shared one, treating the book as a true and honest, albeit not an entirely factual depiction of her own life. For as Romano would later affirm, any alterations or reinventions did not "change the *truth* of the book, which does not (ever) consist in its *truthfulness*".

Biographical details in *A Silence Shared* are therefore never "givens", and it is worth considering one such detail as it appears in the very first pages: "I had work to do in those weeks, a classic to translate. I sank into it like something that was outside of time, which calmed me." In 1943, the writer Cesare Pavese, a

7

former university classmate of Romano, asked her to translate Flaubert's *Three Tales* for the publishing house Einaudi, where he was as an editor. This unnamed classic, referenced infrequently and seemingly in passing, bears an understated importance, not only because Romano uses it to introduce the theme of sinking into *a time outside of time*, which plays out in the novel as a whole. The period depicted in *A Silence Shared*, in fact, overlaps with a creative process that leads directly to the birth of the prose writer and novelist. Romano described translating Flaubert as nothing short of life-changing: "The translation of this simple and essential prose allowed me to realize that prose can be just as rigorous as poetry, that prose and poetry are, rather, the same thing. 'A Simple Heart' was decisive for me: the end of the prejudice I had against the novel. I also owe to Flaubert my shift from painting to narrative."

Translation, this interpretive art, is truly at the heart of the book, a fact evidenced in Romano's ability to take the silences, the subtle actions and the spare words of the four protagonists, and have them assume deeper shades of meaning for the reader. They speak to us in the more universal language of hidden intentions, of profound and often conflicting emotions, of gestures both realized and implied—communication that primarily exists in the unsaid. "Where there is love / even silence / is word", Romano wrote in her posthumously published *Diario ultimo* (Last Diary), and the transformation of silence into word is one of the principal artistic feats accomplished in these pages.

In reality, Romano translated not one, but two classics during the war: after Flaubert, she turned to the painter Eugène

Delacroix's journal (Adolfo Ruata, a translator himself, would find a publisher), a project that left a similarly profound mark. Romano, who would publish multiple travel journals and diaries over the decades, consistently employed in her prose a diarylike intimacy and immediacy of expression, while simultaneously incorporating internal debate and dialogue, including parenthetical reconsiderations and asides. A striking example is the reflexive question presented after Giulia first encounters Paolo: "I felt as though he didn't even see me, that his—blind?—eyes were seeing something behind me, through me." Formal elements such as these, which seem natural for a diarist though quietly startling in a novel, reveal Romano's approach to writing as a gradual and never-finished process of "seeing the truth within myself", to use again the words of Giulia. Nevertheless, the book that offers the clearest counterpart to *A Silence Shared* is the one Romano had most recently translated, Béatrix Beck's tale of infatuation set during the German occupation and the French Resistance, *Léon Morin, prêtre*. The existential and political discussions that fill Beck's book grant an impression of the different shape Romano might have given to her own Resistance novel, had she not decided after the initial stages of writing to substitute longer discussions with brief, pregnant lines and to leave the "frequent and endless" conversations "unsaid" on the page, as she wrote in her afterword.

Finally, translation is key to Romano's writing, and to *A Silence Shared* in particular, as an art of transition, of *carrying over*, with the novel happily inhabiting a liminal space between mediums. Just as Romano saw the book as something between prose and poetry, the most notable Italian poets of her day, from Eugenio Montale to Pier Paolo Pasolini, described her novels as essentially poetry in prose. The lyric rhythm of the text is informed by a musical conception of the power of silence and pauses when effectively placed amid sound and noise, a dynamic mirrored in the way the suspended, snow-muffled atmosphere that forms around the couples is intermittently disrupted by the war. In an introductory note to her book *Le lune di Hvar* (The Moons of Hvar) Romano would describe this distilled quality of her prose in the following terms: "The words have to be few, between spaces and silences: that way they live." The novel also occupies a transitional state as regards Romano's relation to the visual arts and to the silent art of painting. Although she displays an innate eye for visual description, the book is hardly a descriptive novel in the traditional sense; her painterly talent is instead in finding a stillness that, like Old Masters paintings, captures the exact moment of unspoken revelation. This revelatory dimension even becomes overt in the novel's few direct references to the art form: when Ada "looked like a painting that shone for an instant", no longer seeming herself "but Ada as goddess, as sacred dancer, revealed by a light reflected off the wall of a dark temple"; or at the dinner table in Tetto Murato, where "everything livened up again, after freezing in dismay, like a tableau vivant that had truly come to life".

Romano continued to implement visual elements in her work—in 1975 she produced her first "visual novel" in which photographs are conceived as the text and the accompanying words as illustrations—and although she abandoned painting during the war, Romano the visual artist still exists, quite literally, in these pages. The manuscripts are full of drawings, especially female nudes and faces in profile. Female models were a common subject of study at Casorati's school, but as the handwritten words move between and become submerged in these figures, it is impossible not to recall that Romano's novel, while ethereal, is one of attraction and the body: the beautiful body of Ada, the comforting physicality of Stefano ("Stefano's dry body smelled good, the smell of bread fresh from the oven") and, of course, the sick body of Paolo, whose very malady becomes beguiling, mystifying—in other words, another source of attraction.

Another silence present in the novel, and to a certain extent in Romano's life, is her silence regarding her involvement in the antifascist struggle. Romano consistently downplayed any direct involvement in the Resistance, preferring not "to talk of personal undertakings", as she said in the interviews gathered in *L'eterno presente* (The Eternal Present), though she added that taking action was a necessity: "In important moments, you have no choice. Even if one is an artist, one is also a citizen." Adolfo Ruata was a key figure in the Partito d'Azione in Cuneo, and their close relationship during the Resistance—and the severe risks of helping to protect such a figure—points to Romano's engagement. An early chapter with handwritten edits reveals that Romano originally considered making Giulia's political role more explicit, portraying it similarly to how she would later describe her own involvement: "Faced with the alternatives of history, she, too, was a partisan; but of political action she felt annoyance and, almost, shame, though she knew that in that moment it was her duty." Even if Paolo is the only true partisan in the finished novel, this undisclosed element of the author's life is perhaps another reason why Giulia and Paolo's mysterious affinity is so strong, and why they seem "made to understand each other".

Clearly uninterested in using her writing as a tool for self-aggrandizement, Romano was no more interested in aggrandizing the actions of others, and the fact that the novel didn't celebrate the Resistance more directly attracted some criticism following its publication in 1957—Giulia's narration even alludes obliquely to how the leftist ideals of the Resistance, and the people who fought for them, were in many ways abandoned in post-war Italy. But the Resistance and the war more generally are by no means secondary or an accidental backdrop. On the contrary, it is the large-scale historical event itself that forces the characters into a kind of exile from daily life, as they develop a deeper and unrepeatable form of solidarity through their common hopes for the future. This can be understood as the last and most essential silence in the novel, namely, the suspension of what the characters consider to be normal life, the hushed anticipation of what will come "after". But as the war ends and a return to the everyday begins, Tetto Murato, along with the exceptional relationships that were shaped there, inevitably transforms into a thing of the past, an unreachable and legendary period that, like childhood itself, was nevertheless lived firsthand. There is a suggestion of this return to childhood in Romano's fictionalization of herself and the other real-life figures, since she named the characters Giulia and Ada after Eugenia and Adolfo's two daughters, who were young girls at the time of the war.

The depiction of events that emerges is therefore metaphysical, dreamlike, with an atmosphere verging on fairytale, and yet realistic. To read letters between Romano and the Ruatas from the time is to be presented with all the truth of the novel, which ultimately proves to be an authentic snapshot of people and their temperaments in the face of war and illness: Eugenia who, like Ada, shows joyful assurance even in dire circumstances; Adolfo, with his restrained yet palpable affection for Romano. Most remarkably, even the seemingly mystical element of living in a time outside of time was truly an experience shared. In April 1945, on the eve of the Italian liberation—when the characters, too, would separate in *A Silence Shared*—Adolfo confessed in a letter to Romano that the "days that you were here now seem to me so short, and different from all the rest, and most of all that they are outside of time; in the way that everything that belongs to memory is, in reality, outside of time, and I mean not only the chronological kind—which doesn't matter—but psychological time, which is the only time, for us".*

* Lalla Romano's epistolary correspondences and the manuscripts of *Tetto Murato* are held in the Fondo Lalla Romano at the Biblioteca Nazionale Braidense in Milan, an extensive archive that was donated to the library by Antonio Ria, Romano's dedicated companion during the last decade and a half of her life. In addition to Mr Ria and the Braidense, I would like to express my thanks to PEN America for helping to support this translation through the PEN Grant for the English Translation of Italian Literature.

*The only true silence
is a silence shared.*

CESARE PAVESE

I

I had heard people talk about them, the way locals talk about out-of-towners: as something suspicious, if not outright scandalous.

He, a teacher and intellectual, sent to that isolated town near the border as if in a kind of exile; she, proud, aristocratic. No one knew how they managed to get by: they didn't give lessons, and yet no one could say they had racked up any debts. Worst of all was that they "didn't go to church".

I had felt bad for these strangers. For them, life in that provincial town could not have been easy.

One day, a woman was pointed out to me on the balcony of a new house built over the old fortified walls—I knew it had to be her.

There was an ancient grace to this figure as she carried out the dancelike act of hanging laundry on a clothesline. Squeezed into a robe which opened out like a bell, she twirled rapidly with abrupt, even haughty movements; her hair she wore knotted at the top of her head.

I stood looking at her, mesmerized, and I was sorry when she went back inside.

On a small bench, her young daughter still sat clutching a doll. There was something ancient about her, too; maybe her long, very fair hair, which fell down over her little shoulders.

What came over me then was almost pity, a desire to protect her.

I too felt lost in that town, where I had spent my childhood, no less: my return had been forced by the war.

I lived in the now unfamiliar house of two elderly cousins of my mother. The cousins had been beautiful in their youth, and still were now that they were old, or nearly old. Stefano, my husband, regarded them admiringly, subtly paying his respects; they were grateful for the way he treated them like ladies. They listened attentively—slightly rigid—as he told of wartime life in Turin.

As for me, Stefano's brief visits shook me, and left me feeling weaker.

The cousins had set up a gloomy room for us, their mother's old sitting room. The only option was to stay put on the bed, in that room cramped with furniture and other useless things, which moreover happened to be freezing cold. The bed, located in the middle of the room, was tall and had a bulging "bombé" frame. It wasn't a double bed, and even for two skinny people it was tight.

Stefano would lie stretched out; he stayed composed while he slept as long as he didn't have bad dreams.

He liked the summer, sleeping sheetless as though in a field. I, on the other hand, liked a winter bed. In the summer and in the winter Stefano's dry body smelled good, the smell of bread fresh from the oven, I used to say. But now it was hard to find that warm aroma again: always too much cold had been endured. His feet were icy, and in his hair lingered the sad smell of trains from his journey there.

I had work to do in those weeks, a classic to translate. I sank into it like something that was outside of time, which calmed me.

When people came to see the cousins, I would put away the book, the dictionaries and notebooks, and I'd flip through issues of *Pro Familia*, bound by year. (I stayed in there with them because it was the only heated room.) That magazine, with its photographs of high-ranking clergymen, was no less gloomy than the visits.

The visitors were elderly women, the widows of generals and the like: gossipy and piously narrow-minded.

The cousins listened without interruption. They didn't enquire into other people's business. Not that they were particularly easy-going; they just avoided indiscretion.

Sometimes, if the woman talking was more colourful, I listened too. That was how I heard about Ada and Paolo. The woman was telling a story about them: an example, she said, of "punished unbelief" and "divine retribution".

The story went back a couple of years, to when "they" had arrived in town with their baby daughter who was only a few months old. The baby did not "even" have a necklace with a medallion of the Madonna around her neck, so the wet nurse secretly pinned a medallion to her shirt. The baby ended up swallowing the medallion. The doctor couldn't figure out the

17

problem and kept tormenting the child, who was eventually saved, when she was on the verge of dying, by a doctor in Turin.

If a story just like that one—dying babies, divine retribution—had come back to me from childhood memories, it would have seemed fantastical, unreal. Now I found it frightening for the meaning its narrator gave it. I saw no greatness in their God.

II

I was walking alone under the porticoes; I passed by a young woman with a long stride who didn't look like she was from around there. I glimpsed her eyes flashing at me, something black and light blue. I recognized her, called after her. She froze for a moment; I told her that I'd been hoping to meet her, that I was also from Turin. Her expression immediately changed, and, smiling, she invited me to come to her house the next day.

In the house I mostly noticed a rather large, shadowy painting. Under a big feathered hat, a pale woman's face peered out with a dark look in her eyes, sad as if in reproach.

"Paolo's mother," she said. "She was *such* a beautiful woman."

I compared her uplifted, luminous face with the waxen face of the woman in the painting. She added almost nonchalantly, though firmly, too: "It's all we have left from Paolo's house. It was *such* a lavish house." I smiled to myself for all of those "suches", which evoked a world both naïve and absolute, although it wasn't lost on me that she was at all times referring to the past.

Other paintings, English-style ink drawings: all of it had come from his house.

So, they had no other home but this one. They, perhaps, did not have anyone left.

It was different for Stefano and me: our homes and families were still there. But we had left without well-made and austere pieces of furniture or paintings.

They had grieved losses that, in some way, continued to haunt them. That face in the painting loomed slightly over everything. "She was very unhappy," she said, seeing that I was looking at it again. "She was ill."

With these words, it sounded as though she were trying to justify something: her own harshness, or the other woman's? But she didn't say anything else.

The little girl waited, standing by the door, her hair looking like strands of light. Her mother went to pull out a drawer and gave it to her "to put back in order".

I watched the girl, who with chubby, light hands, silently placed the objects in piles and in lines. At a certain point she said, "I've finished." Her mother took the drawer as it was—which is to say, with the items arranged in meticulous disorder—and went to put it back, as if that were the one and only way it had to be. Still unsatisfied, the girl asked, "Now what?"

Her mother sighed quickly (lovingly), then opened a cupboard and handed the girl a tea set to play with. The cups were nearly transparent; surely, they were also from their former home. I hazarded asking whether there was any danger of her breaking them. She looked somewhat sombre and amazed as she turned to me: "Why, of course not!"

While watching the girl, the story I'd heard about her came back to me.

I usually felt embarrassed making other people talk to me about their misfortunes, but I thought I needed to bring it up. (I knew that illnesses for a family are like battles for a general.) Ada, bent over her sewing, suddenly reared up her head; then, without complaint, she jumped right into the story.

There were no medallions involved (something the pious old woman had made up)—the baby had swallowed a safety pin. Beyond that detail, the new version of the story was essentially the same as the first.

Out of all that emotion, one image was left stuck in my head: racing in the car towards Turin on a snowy day, with the dying baby in her arms. But this time, despite my disinclination for that kind of sob story, I felt something edifying in it, which lulled the soul.

When she finished telling me the story, she declared, "I simply understood that there is such a thing as providence."

It was not just a manner of speaking. I saw, as in an allegory, her victory and the confusion of the pious hags.

III

I started to go to their house often. She was enormously inter-ested in the circumstances of my life, which were ordinary. She spoke of her own life in fragments, through allusions, like it was all well-known and yet mysterious. Her husband, for instance. She talked about him as if I'd always known him, but also as if she herself was not sure she really understood the man.

I went along with her, to the extent that I didn't naturally feel the need to ask questions.

She alluded to what Paolo would do "after", as though to something secret and at the same time legendary. Back then, a new life was supposed to begin for everyone, after. But she seemed to imply that there was something else, too: "another" obstacle which in the future would cease to stand in their way. When she would reference this enemy, different from the one we all shared, I thought I caught her glancing now and then at the woman in the painting, as if at someone who was generally in the know.

Since her husband was always "in there"—in the study—I went out on a limb and asked what he was working on. She gave me one of her outraged replies: "I don't know!" Then she settled down and, sounding joyfully mischievous, added, "I'd like to know what he does," before wrapping up in her usual definitive tone: "Paolo shares with me so little of what he thinks, and tells me so little of what he does." Then she smiled again, and I thought she did so in order not to say that there was, in fact, one way he communicated with her.

When I met him, he seemed even more secretive than I could have imagined.

We were in the entrance hall, light falling from the lamp onto his upturned face as he quietly closed the door behind him. It was a face with large features, vigorous but tired. He shook my hand without any trace of warmth. I felt as though he didn't even see me, that his—blind?—eyes were seeing something behind me, through me. The next time there were also other people over. He was sitting upright, as in a portrait from the nineteenth century: one leg crossed over the other and arms folded.

He didn't speak—I knew this, too, that he "left people wanting"—but his half-closed eyes glimmered behind his glasses.

I had already gathered that he liked to tease. She had told me that he would make ironic comments about our conversations: "Do you talk about literature? And what about politics?"

She had even warned me in advance about what always happened: that when someone met him, they lost interest in her. I had no intention of following the norm. In fact, I was already trying to circumscribe the mystery of this man, with its many trademarks, from his silence around others, to the books

I always found flipped face down with such clear intention that I didn't dare reach out to turn them over, as I easily would have done in any other home.

Soon enough, he began gracing us with his presence—for the most part, a silent one—when it was time for tea. That was when I realized that the smile I'd seen in his eyes around other people was not due to those people or to their conversations, as I'd thought: it was for her. She was what he found so amusing. Her sudden bursts, the way she would get upset, or enthusiastic, over nothing.

That teasing smile of his was also sweet, tender; and yet to me it seemed to have something cold to it, for the very fact that he was amused in the first place.

I had chosen Stefano to marry instead of one of my literary peers because I had found natural in him the things that they went looking for in books to make themselves alluring. Now, Paolo was definitely literary, but he was almost a different species, maybe from a different era. He didn't resemble my old companions in any way, but he was also the opposite of Stefano, who was so open and trusting of life.

When he didn't smile, when he was absorbed in thought—his eyes again looking blind—it was as though Paolo were cut off, protected. But he seemed to be ashamed of this, so clear was his kindness in breaking out of his isolation to talk to us.

Stefano found Paolo was exactly as he had expected; but Ada managed—as she did with everyone—to surprise him.

As for her, she first saw Stefano when he was at his most defenceless, talking to their daughter. The girl was standing by the front entrance in that quizzical way of hers. Stefano bent down next to her, lifting with two fingers the large beads of her sky-blue necklace and lightly touching her silken strands of hair. When he stood back up, Ada was there too, and she had that smile which she seemed to be unaware of.

Ada found out that Stefano had a knack for recounting events—she had *such* fun listening to stories, and Paolo would never humour her. Not that Stefano wasn't secretive, in a certain (intimate) way; but he didn't mind sharing his own evolving view of the world, and he was happy to be a part of what he discovered along the way. (Maybe he even narrated to himself, like everyone who loves to tell stories.)

I wasn't able, as he was, to mature by learning from things as they happened; I preferred abstract shortcuts. That's partly why the war—that happening like no other—was so loathsome to me. What's more, I was no good at listening: I would interrupt with questions and, even worse, I always wanted to know what was going to happen next, trying to guess the ending.

Ada sat looking focused and serious while Stefano told his stories, which he must have loved.

He told her—Ada had asked him to—about how he had helped haul the bodies from under the rubble in his neighbourhood. I too became pulled in by the story and, like Ada, I watched his long hands: he moved them as he spoke, his fingers slightly stiff.

Every so often Ada let out a quick cry, clasped her hands together, and opened her eyes wide before shutting them again;

when that happened, my gaze would meet Paolo's wicked eyes behind his glasses.

The two of them were always the ones to talk—Stefano and Paolo had understood each other (man to man) in very few words—and when the conversation shifted to food and costs, Ada went to get her expenditure notebook to show it to Stefano. The notebook was so precise and orderly that Stefano couldn't help but smile. At that point, she jumped abruptly to her feet and squeezed the notebook to her chest with two hands, like a schoolgirl jealously hiding her notes.

IV

On the 25th of July, Stefano and I were out in the valleys (it was during Stefano's vacation), and we heard the news from an old country priest.[*] We had thought that he was unwell when we saw him a little out of breath, peering worriedly at the road, so we offered to give him a hand. The priest told us the news, but he didn't believe it; he was shaking his head, waiting for other people to confirm it. He had found out from a peasant woman who had come up from the village.

At the house, my mother's cousins, who had never been fascists, made subdued comments, as if it were an everyday occurrence.

I immediately went with Stefano to find our friends. Ada had gone out with their daughter; cigarette smoke and the soft, excited hum of discussions came from the half-opened door to the study.

Paolo appeared with a cigarette between his fingers. Only that single, out-of-the-ordinary detail—him smoking—gave away his emotion. He apologized with his usual kindness for

_____

[*] On July 25, 1943, Benito Mussolini, after receiving a vote of no confidence from the Fascist Grand Counil, was removed from power.

Ada's absence, and for having "some friends" in there with him. He took a piece of paper out of his jacket pocket and handed it to Stefano to read: it was a draft of a proclamation about the war.

I had expected more joy, and so I was disappointed. I felt irked, and a little bit jealous.

Everyone developed absurd hopes that summer: it was natural for Ada to treat them as solid facts. During Paolo's silences, though, I would notice her giving him looks full of concern, almost fear.

In August, Stefano told us about the horrors of other bombings. (At night, the glimmering of the fires burning in Turin could be seen from the cousins' roof.)

He had frightening dreams while sleeping next to me: he saw armed raids in the houses, he heard shouts in the night. He would moan, and I'd wake him; he'd twist around some more now that he was awake, and say: "I was about to find out who they were, what it was." But Stefano was calm when it was time to leave again—he was happy that he alone had to go, it seemed right to him—and his goodbyes gave me courage.

Once, when going back to the city, he left me with Ada and Paolo, who wanted me to stay with them a little while longer. They knew that it was a difficult moment for me to get through.

But almost right away, Paolo said that he was tired, and he went back into his study. I stayed with Ada in the bedroom.

There was nothing in the world I wanted, I felt empty. The

sun had just set, and the room was filled with a soft light and a warm colour. Ada was lying down on the bed. I was looking at her, contemplating her beauty, which seemed almost incorporeal, almost "risen from the sea"—to the point that, maybe, with a simple touch, she would come undone.

I was startled when she suddenly jumped up and ran off. There was a rough hissing sound, which I only noticed after she had already left the room. She returned almost immediately and, with a somewhat wild movement, went back to her spot on the other side of the bed, her arms arched behind her head as before. She didn't say anything, but each time the hissing came back, she nodded as if she recognized it and approved (or rather, accepted the hissing, since there was no getting rid of it).

Now I could hear too the sound of rhythmic steps coming and going, quickly. Ada sighed, and smiled at me: "I'm sorry." And then: "Do you want to see?" She stretched out her arm and gently pushed open the door next to the bed. From where I was, I saw Paolo wrapped in a large black cloak, like a bandit from a fairytale, pacing feverishly up and down the hallway.

"Walking helps him," Ada explained. I must have looked scared, because she tried to reassure me. "It's only asthma," she said.

V

I wasn't in town on the 8th of September, either. As soon as I got back, I hurried on my bicycle to look for Ada and Paolo.[*]

They had left a message saying that I could find them on the "old road" to Borgo.

I saw them at a turn in the country road between the mulberry hedges, in the already soft autumnal light, holding their daughter's hand. They looked like an image of happiness that was already far away in time.

While I was getting off my bicycle, a group of deserters caught up to us: tired, dragging their heavy feet. They passed us by without saying a word, looking proud like guilty men.

Not long after, we saw another soldier sitting hunched over on the side of the road. He lifted his head to show us a face with big, sad eyes like a child's. There was no fear of offending him by looking at him.

---

[*] On September 8, 1943, Italy's surrender to the Allies was announced. Germany swiftly occupied northern and much of central Italy, rescuing Mussolini from prison and propping up the puppet government of Salò. Partisan Resistance groups continued to fight Fascist and Nazi forces until the liberation of the country was finally completed in the spring of 1945.

Ada began asking questions: he replied that he'd had enough, and that either way he couldn't possibly go on like that, in his uniform. He spoke with the objective tone of someone at the end of his rope, but who was also humble, naïve. He had probably never left the nest before the war: in his state of dereliction, he still had a hint of childish innocence about him.

The soldier shuffled along sheepishly once Ada invited him to follow us: we could reach the house without drawing any attention to ourselves. At the house they gave him new clothes, dressing him from head to toe in Paolo's things (all of it irreplaceable).

Paolo and Ada acted then the way they always did, except Ada was uncharacteristically cool-tempered; there was none of the agitation that usually attends giving things away or making sacrifices. They shook the runaway's hand; he thanked them just as simply, and promised he would return everything to them. Paolo said that it wasn't a good idea. He said this calmly, normally, as though stating the obvious, but I suddenly considered how much uncertainty was, by now, stretching out before us.

Ada was getting something ready, feverishly. Paolo needed to leave. He had been seen on his bicycle, a rolled up blanket on the handlebars, heading towards the valleys, and they were looking for him. Then he was forced to turn back, since he'd had a fit of asthma.

I found this out from Ada, who seemed most upset over his sense of humiliation, for the fact that he "wasn't like the rest".

31

But she didn't let her emotions get the better of her: she became hardened, visibly so, when necessary.

At the last second Paolo addressed me in an oddly cere-monious, humble manner, which hurt me: "I would be much obliged to you," he said, "if you could find a place for Ada and the girl to sleep tonight. I'm worried they'll frighten the two of them. I was warned." He placed a small envelope in my hand. "Please, take this too. It's just a little bit of money. Thank you."

He shook my hand with his sweet and wry smile from the good times; he tried to kid around, saying, "I'm hunted like a dog," as if reciting a line from a joke. Then he hugged Ada. I didn't want to look at them, but I did in time to realize that she was trembling.

VI

I thought I would ask the cousins about the room.

The fact that I spent time at Ada and Paolo's house—a fact never openly disapproved of, or rather, one hardly ever mentioned—had ended up cooling, I could clearly sense, the meagre confidence they had put in me.

When I asked them to host Ada, they didn't say no, but they did look very surprised. I felt discouraged, and didn't dare insist.

Ada consoled me, finding for herself reasons to justify the cousins' behaviour. But I wasn't listening, I was mortified.

I didn't hold a grudge against the cousins: in the end I decided that it had only been a sort of shyness on their part. It did prove to me, however, that it was not a bad idea to "keep the two worlds separate"—the very rule I had chosen to follow in the first place.

After that, I felt Ada's gaze rest on me with a particular weight to it. She thought that I had given some incredible proof of friendship by asking the cousins for that favour. In fact, we did become closer friends. This didn't mean telling each other more; if anything it made it less and less necessary for us to explain ourselves or to share secrets.

*

Paolo sent his letters for Ada to me, since the cousins' address wouldn't draw suspicion. I would look at my name, which he had traced on the envelope in tiny letters with his sharp handwriting; I felt that he couldn't have not given a thought, if only an involuntary one, to the person whose name that was.

In any event, I resented the people who weren't around and were far away (maybe out of a kind of defence mechanism). I felt this—and much more—towards Stefano, too. When he was there, this resentment would mix with my joy and turn it violent, nearly bitter.

Stefano's visits became rarer, problematic even, since his work had been moved much farther away, to another city.

The first phase of our time apart, which had been so hard for me, now seemed lucky and almost happy.

VII

At a certain point, I missed Ada, too.

It began in the summer when she found friends of hers from Turin, whom she apparently held in high regard. A lawyer, or something of that sort, and his wife. The lawyer had been called to duty with the title of Major.

I was introduced to them. She had the bored, distant demeanour of someone who was "born with a silver spoon in her mouth," whereas he was attentive, considerate. The Major was a good deal smaller than his wife, who clearly called the shots in their relationship; he would look to her before speaking and, when she spoke, listen admiringly. Both of them expressed discreetly, though not without condescension, their obvious opinions. I was suspicious of them, that they had been obedient followers of the regime; but I never succeeded in getting Ada to admit as much.

The worst part was that I became jealous of the affection Ada showed them. Especially when, upon their arrival, I would hear her excitedly exclaim the same way she did when greeting me. I didn't like to see Ada and that woman together. Ada with her fervour; the other stolid, merely obliging. When compared to this real noblewoman—or presumably real, at least going by the rules—it suddenly stood out to me how Ada was an aristocrat of the imagination, a Grand Duchess from a fairytale.

When Ada finally asked me if I didn't like the Fantonis, I more or less confessed my impression of them. Smiling as she did whenever she had got to the bottom of something—a smile that was slightly enchanted, and yet subtle, mischievous—she said, "I expected as much." I wanted to know why. "Paolo says the same thing."

I was relieved—actually, I felt strong, and from that moment on I could think of the Fantonis without any jealousy. The 8th of September had transformed the Major into a civilian, after which the Fantonis disappeared into the countryside. When they found out that Paolo had gone to Turin, they tried to convince Ada to share the place where they'd taken refuge. Ada accepted.

Later I found out that they lived extremely close to Signora Sibilla, and that she had actually been the one to help them find the house, a hovel of a place.

The Fantonis had come to know people in town, and they took advantage of these connections; since Sibilla lived in the country, they had gone to visit her. There they must have sung the praises of her refuge, her unkempt garden, her mangy and unfriendly cat, the depressingly gloomy surroundings. Because presumably it had all been according to a plan, one that was innocent enough: they just happened to be looking for a "good opportunity" to escape the bombings.

I smiled to myself at the thought of this pairing. I had known Signora Sibilla since I was a little girl.

Not that Signora Sibilla wasn't, as they said, "from a good family". But she had been a rebel, an independent spirit, and I was sure that even as an old woman she would not be a good match for the Fantonis, and much less so the Fantonis for her.

Ada and I rarely saw each other. When she came into town, I kept her company on my bicycle for a portion of her walk back; but I never made it all the way to the house.

Beyond town, the riverbanks—the high, woody stretches along the river—flourished, thick and blooming; and so much beauty seemed like madness, now that the sky was cut through daily by flocks of migrating birds and the town was becoming more and more withdrawn, taciturn, patrolled up and down by the frightening ranks of the Muti brigade.

VIII

I was working on my classic, and to check something at the
National Library—it was open every now and then—I had
to go to Turin. Ada asked me if I planned on going to see Paolo:
I didn't say yes and I didn't say no. She taught me the way to
knock, just in case.

Stefano—before moving—had seen Paolo a few times; they
had even had lunch together. When described by Stefano, Paolo
was less mysterious, more human. They had gone to Firenze,
one of those cafeterias where you could eat if you were "a
card-carrying member". The girls who waited there were beautiful: big, grandiose, classical beauties, but ill-mannered. They
immediately put the food on the table, or to be precise, threw
everything down on the dirty oilcloth before turning around
as though they had placed slop in front of a dog.

The one who served Stefano and Paolo that day was nicer;
she had grey eyes with dark rings around them, high cheekbones
that gave her a bit of a Russian look. Paolo had told Stefano that
"a friend of his was crazy about" that girl.

I went up the five flights of stairs in a dusty building with
chipped walls without passing anyone. I knocked as I was

supposed to, and Paolo opened the door. He looked at me without seeing me or without recognizing me, for what felt like an eternity: his eyes were sunken, far away. Then he recognized me, smiled. He apologized for the mess: the bed was unmade. The landlady didn't always come upstairs to tidy up, and he hadn't made it himself because he had just come back in. There had been a meeting the night before (and so the bed was unmade since the previous day). He had spent the night in a chair.

He relayed this to me in a detached monotone, a voice he used with people he didn't know well and, I imagined, at the school where he taught.

"So you didn't sleep?"

He shrugged. "I never sleep anyway."

I didn't feel any sympathy: frankly, I was mean. Maybe the resentment towards those who weren't around was still at work in me. I thought—I rewrote in my head—that mocking line: "Let me have men about that are fat, such as sleep a-nights."

No one likes the sight of an unmade bed, not even their own. Looking at that dishevelled cot, I was struck by a sudden feeling of pity. In that moment, Paolo—I thought I saw his smile glimmer behind his glasses—invited me to have lunch there with him. I wasn't going to find anything much better, he said, in a cafeteria.

He gave me a book, and asked me to wait: he had to buy a few things.

He had spoken sweetly, as he normally did, but so resolutely, too, that I felt intimidated.

When he came back, he was carrying food wrapped in two small bundles which he placed on the kitchen table; he lit the gas, put the water on the stove. He went about the large empty kitchen making precise movements—taking every item out of a built-in cupboard—and he looked like a chemist preparing an experiment.

When out of one of the wrappings appeared strawberries—already a slightly fabled fruit in itself—I had the exciting impression that there was something "magical" to all of it. I decided it was a good idea to play along and not reveal any amazement.

While I was telling Ada how everything had gone, I suddenly realized that I had been crazy to put so much as a dent in Paolo's scarce provisions, those meagre resources. I was distraught: "I shouldn't have accepted."

Ada didn't contradict me, but she did offer me an excuse: "You couldn't *not* accept." And she added, "I know how he is. You can't say no."

IX

Stefano—travelling partly by train, partly in a truck—had come for Easter. We sat squeezed together, after lunch, on the famous bulging bed, because it was raining and we were cold.

I told him what I knew. Paolo's salary had been suspended, and now the only thing Ada had at her disposal was the little she made giving lessons in a school for displaced people.

I had unlimited faith in Stefano's abilities to resolve all problems, including money-related ones, even if I knew, naturally, that he didn't have much. I simply presented the facts. (*Vinum non habent*.)*

Stefano said that we had a few thousand lire "for any eventuality", and this was one.

He went himself, in the rain, to take it to them. I explained the way up to a point that I knew, then he could ask for directions. I knew the name of the house, or the Tetto, as they were called in those parts.

When he came back, Stefano said that it was a dirty, ramshackle place, where he wouldn't have stayed if you paid him.

---

* "They have no wine." Mary's words to Jesus at the Wedding at Cana (John 2:3).

Later Ada told me about Stefano's visit. "I was alone in the kitchen—it's on the ground floor, big and dark. The Fantonis were sleeping, and our daughter and Domenica had gone over to see some of the locals. I was feeling a little down, maybe because I didn't have anything to do. It was raining. I was looking at the puddle: there's this big puddle under the window that never dries up, and that's when I saw him come around the corner on his bicycle. Not that I saw him all that clearly, but I could tell it was him. When I ran up to meet him, he had already leant his bike against a wall. He was soaking wet; I lit a fire for him. Before he left, he told me why he had come: 'We don't need it. You'll pay us back later.' I told him, 'We have relatives.' He said, 'Some things call for friends, not relatives.'"

In the summer, Ada disappeared for a few weeks. She had informed me beforehand with a note: she was leaving the girl and Domenica with the Fantonis, and was going to Turin. Paolo was sick. To me, sickness mostly meant something that made it difficult, nearly impossible, to communicate with people. Usually, I didn't enquire about illnesses nor ask questions of those afflicted; and besides, in Paolo's case there was little to ask about. I knew from Ada that his malady was, going by what the doctors had said, mysterious. It seemed strange to me that they would admit as much, and I wondered whether Ada's imagination had something to do with it. It wasn't a single ailment, nor was there a prevalent one; as soon as you believed that you could understand it from certain symptoms, others, which had earlier seemed secondary, would reappear, take over.

I didn't receive any news until Ada came back.

She was excited. She essentially skipped over his condition and told me instead about a woman who had taken to protecting Paolo, and who was currently having him stay at her place.

All of this was so unexpected, so out of tune, it actually made me feel uncomfortable with Ada.

I was indignant; I even had the impression that Ada admired that woman because she was rich. I told her so, and Ada, who was getting a kick out of my bad mood, replied, "Well, of course!"

"And what about Paolo? Does he like this woman?" I went so far as to ask.

She didn't answer right away. Then she said gravely, "Most of all, Paolo needs me. But I didn't have a choice."

X

I could never tell if Ada really felt as confident about things as she seemed to. I didn't know if she was really sure that Paolo was doing much better, as she had said upon her return, if she really wasn't worried now that he was alone once more in the city.

I thought that maybe she had truly believed—wished—that Paolo had made a full recovery, when I saw how torn up she was by the news that he was unwell again.

But I realized that hers wasn't full-blown despair (it never was with her). What was torturing her was a specific predicament: would Paolo agree to leave everything behind, and take shelter in the country?

She had let her body collapse onto a chair—a tall walnut stool in the cousins' living room—and she looked fragile, drained of her usual strength, her long arms inert, her head down, bent over her thin neck.

I said to her, "I'll come with you," to help cheer her up. It surprised me that she wasn't surprised by my decision. She had only one thought on her mind.

*

By now it was autumn and the weather had already turned cold. In the rickety train carriage, the windows had no panes. Ada slipped a scarf off her neck and gave it to me to tie under my chin.

In front of us sat a man with a large sack resting between his legs. He was glancing up at us out of the corner of his clever eyes. He had the kind of drooping moustache that was popular in the countryside, but he probably wasn't a farmhand: his face was too candid, too expressive; maybe, I thought, a travelling salesman.

The "man with the sack" threw a hand all the way down, pulled out a large green pear, and offered it to us, jokingly, with a gallant flair, but we didn't dare reach out; then he pulled out another, and holding both in his big hand he repeated the offer. This time we took one each and immediately bit in.

They were cold and sweet, and we still had a little hunger left over after.

The man started offering his pears around to everyone, gesticulating, making a show of himself, in this way dissimulating his kindness. He regarded us as his special favourites whom he had to look after, pulling out from his sack two pears for us every time, and every time he winked as he placed them in our hands, as if to say, "We're friends."

The goodness of this man revived us.

XI

By the time we got there it was almost the start of curfew. We hurried through deserted streets strewn with heaps of rubble, which we had to skirt.

Paolo was living on the ground floor of a building on one of the city's wide avenues. In the feeble blue light of the hallway, he looked so lifeless I feared he wasn't even going to speak. He looked at us almost with hostility, alarmed: "Why did you come?" In her emotion, Ada, failing to come up with anything better, imprudently said, "We came to see you."

Paolo "never" had fits of anger; but his silence could become like ice.

The tension only lasted a second. With rather detached hospitality, he offered to get something ready for dinner. But Ada, happy to spring into action, ran to the kitchen and started cooking the eggs, religiously brought from the country. "You two wait in there," she said.

The room where we sat was square-shaped, with a very high ceiling. A mirror began at the floor and took up a whole wall; the only other piece of furniture was a sideboard carved with griffins, monsters, beasts with ivory eyes. A chandelier hung high in the middle of the room too. I got lost looking at it. A milky glass bowl was concealed within a tangle of metal branches forming numerous irregular triangles, so that the light seemed to emanate from the inside of a plant.

"It's a bachelor pad," Paolo said. "What they call a *garçon-nière*." He laughed, and a feeling of immense peace spread through me. Paolo didn't seem sick.

I thought it would make Ada happy to hear this, and I ran into the kitchen. "He doesn't seem sick to me." Without looking up from the eggs, she sighed: "Unfortunately, I can recognize certain signs." Everything plunged back into mystery.

We ate together in the modestly sized, almost bare dining area. Then Ada suggested we get the beds ready. She slipped into hers and said, with the puffed-up voice of a sleepy child, "Go on talking, I'll listen."

Paolo smiled. "She's already asleep," he said, then called out to her: "Ada! Ada!" I was tired too, but I didn't want Paolo to notice—he hadn't asked me if I felt like sleeping. Inured to terrible insomnia (Ada had told me), he couldn't believe it when others were visibly sleepy. He would smile at Ada's sleepiness as if it were a particular privilege of hers, and one of her ingenuous quirks.

My own drowsiness soon stopped pestering me; I had a dull pain in my temples, but I felt clear-headed, excited as though from an adventure. I was amazed that I could so easily go toe to toe with Paolo's famed insomnia. There was a deep silence. We kept our voices down as we spoke, even if noises never bothered Ada when she slept.

Giving a slight sigh of surprise, Ada sat up in her bed. "You two are still up?" Then she went on, "Paolo, let Giulia rest. She's tired. And you too, see if you can rest a bit." She said all of this in one breath, like a little girl afraid of forgetting her lines in a play; then, taking a deeper breath, almost a groan, she fell back down.

Paolo laughed, but he stood up and I followed him.

There was a small room off to the side, taken up almost entirely by an ottoman, and separated not by a door but by a curtain of worn fabric. After coming from the light of snow-covered woods in the other room, the lightbulb's yellow glare felt too harsh. It revealed the disorder of a theatre dressing room: dusty lampshades, a shelf crammed with jars and cans. I became mesmerized looking at a 1919 print. It depicted a thin and mannish woman in a petticoat trying on a military beret in the mirror, with a long cigarette holder between her teeth: the cigarette smoke drew the profile of a dolled-up, feminine young man.

"Amazing how sins age!" Paolo said.

It could have been the exhaustion, the excitement, but everything then seemed wondrous, unreal, like when one dreams and is aware of dreaming. While drawing back the curtain, Paolo turned to say goodnight to me, and I thought that, maybe, it had been beautiful for him too.

XII

We were walking up a road in the hills towards the villa of Signora Borla, the woman who had been looking after Paolo.

Ada—Paolo was walking between us in silence—kept darting alarmed glances at me. I looked at Paolo: his facial expression was that of someone who, rather than suffering, was stunned by the pain. Suddenly he picked up the pace, as though forgetting about us. Ada called out to him. He seemed not to hear. Then she slid an arm under his and signalled for me to do the same. I felt dread and almost an aversion to touching his somewhat stiff arm, with him unaware of it.

The road rose along the bottom of a woody, enclosed valley, with enough humidity in the air to choke on. The sky was overcast, dark. Paolo was breathing heavily, and he was sweating profusely from his forehead as if from enormous physical exertion. Suddenly, giving a start as though waking up, he broke free. "What are you doing? I'm not an invalid, you know." I furtively drew my hand away, and Ada, her voice cracking, said, "Of course—you're great. We were letting you lead us, because we don't know the way." "The way?"

He was having trouble remembering, and he was clearly irritated.

We heard the crunching of gravel: the woman, who had come out to greet us, was at the front gate of her property. She was very small, imperious; she was wearing trousers and gripped between her fingers a long cigarette holder, which she chewed on every so often with horselike teeth. She shook, quite frequently, her mop of bleached hair. At lunch I had more than a little fun observing Ada. The woman talked a lot, flaunting her familiarity with Paolo. For me this was all perfectly fine, since it wasn't my place to speak anyway. Ada took part in the conversation with only glances and exaggerated nods; speaking was not currently an option for her. She was eating without interruption, helping herself to multiple servings of each dish, though nevertheless with haughtiness, taking little bites, her elbows squeezed to her sides. And all of this had, for me, a very comical effect.

Paolo pointed her out to me with his eyes, as if to say, "Don't miss out on the fun." Because it was clear—to us—that Ada was acting according to a plan. She really was hungry, but she was used to eating little, next to nothing actually, to the point that Paolo often scolded her and she would cover up the sacrifices she made with lines like "I already ate," or "You know I don't like how that tastes." Now she was "taking advantage" of the situation; which is to say that she was loading up on food precisely in preparation for future fasts.

It seemed that the woman almost didn't know how to react: maybe, in an obscure way, she sensed Ada was getting the better of her.

After lunch, Ada put her all into the conversation; she was truly grateful to this woman, and felt bad that she had to cause her displeasure in taking Paolo away. I didn't contribute; I was contemplating from my armchair the enormous roosters, the fish, the sailing ships displayed on the furniture. I noticed Ada's eyes on me, and they seemed to be expressing astonishment. I thought I was missing something and that Ada wanted to cue me in; but I felt little curiosity for that house and that woman.

When we left, she walked with us for some of the way through the park; Ada and I walked ahead, she and Paolo behind us. Ada turned around rapidly, then whispered to me, the way little girls do when they've uncovered something forbidden about grownups: "She's jealous."

When the three of us were alone and we began to sink into silence, Ada came out and said it.

"She's jealous, isn't she?"

Paolo sighed. "Now of Giulia, too."

"Oh, is she?" Ada replied, excited, amused. Paolo didn't say any more, and she kept talking. "No surprise there. Giulia made *such* an impression on her."

"And if she didn't so much as look at me?"

"She understood the way you are."

"The way I am?"

"I watched you too. That's it: you're 'different'. And in that house it was even clearer to see. I don't know how to express what I mean, but that's it."

"You've expressed yourself beautifully," Paolo concluded.

I decided to leave that night, because I was afraid the cousins would worry. Ada and Paolo would leave the next day; there was someone Paolo still needed to see.

When we said goodbye, Paolo, turning up his face like a blind man, offered me a hand that had grown cold, with one of those hollow gestures that made him resemble a robot. Afterwards, standing in the stock car, among the crowd of labourers cursing the fact that the train hadn't left yet, I thought back on the words Paolo had said a little earlier, while he was still looking alive and even cheerful.

"So, you'll come," Ada had ventured; she was on pins and needles, fearing that Paolo would refuse at the last minute to abandon "his work". Paolo had replied, "Yes, so long as Giulia comes every day to see me."

I had thought he was joking, but then Ada said seriously, "Of course she'll come. You know how good she is."

Then she shook my hand, and I understood that what she was saying was "thank you".

XIII

A development played in my favour; firstly, because it matched my own superstition about coincidences (I saw them as confirming the necessity of what I was already going to do), and then, because it allowed me to present the idea as something reasonable to the cousins. Both Ada and I found work in schools; I was busy in the morning, whereas she was in the afternoon, which meant we could "take turns by his sickbed".

I would eat and then immediately set out, since I had a long way to go. But at the corner of the piazza, I would stop to buy roasted chestnuts; because I was still hungry, and because I liked them and especially liked eating them along my walk.

In a nook between two pillars, an old woman bundled up in rags, but nevertheless solemn, sibyl-like, had set up her roaster. Ever since I was little I had always seen that old woman—or one just like her—surrounded in the autumn and the winter by a crowd of soldiers: the Alpini in their short greyish-green capes. Their boots would screech on the stone, and the aroma of the chestnuts would mix with the pungent smell of wet cloth and leather.

Now the barracks along the main street leading out of town from the piazza were dismantled, empty; converted, in part, to prisons. Here and there, from the windows with no panes, a young man looked out in his regular country clothing; someone, to add a touch more sadness, would be singing.

I'd stop shelling chestnuts as I passed before them, hurrying my pace.

Crossing the towering bridge was thrilling. Below, emptiness; and, while walking forward, the mountains rising up, moving towards you.

There was a checkpoint at the end of the bridge: a camouflage tent, in front of which an armed soldier paced up and down. I passed by unhurriedly, chewing my chestnuts.

The main road led uphill towards the valleys. I'd turn onto an older side road, the kind that reach out-of-the-way farmsteads and run by the hamlets scattered along the flat stretches of land between the town and the mountains.

The few chestnuts still left to take from the paper cone were nearly all spoiled, mouldy, bitter tasting: they, too, products of wartime. I sank my teeth into them cautiously, spitting out the bitter parts and chewing, slowly, the good ones.

Having emptied the cone, I would try to clean my fingers with the water from a stream—which cleaned nothing—and wipe them with a handful of dry poplar leaves which left a nice smell on my hands, a hint of spring that was hardly there at all.

From the country road I would turn onto another grassier road, really more of a path; at certain points it squeezed between heaps of stones covered in brambles, before becoming muddy, or crowded with big rocks. There were lines of mulberry trees in the surrounding fields, or scattered walnut and apple trees. It was the kind of tightfisted beauty born of poverty.

On the highest branches of the apple trees I would eye a few forgotten fruits, gleaming red; sometimes a fallen apple shimmered on top of the dirt in the field amid the sparse strands of newly sprouted wheat. Then I would look around me like a thief, climb over the low hedge, and run into the field. If a growling dog caught sight of me, my heart would leap into my throat; I'd hide the apple—always a tiny thing—in my hand.

I knew that when the road is long, somewhere after the midpoint there comes a moment of weariness, of discouragement—and that it usually coincides with the most solitary, the most abandoned point in the road.

For me it would occur when I reached a low, dilapidated house, black with soot. It looked like no one lived in it, yet an old and raucous dog would still jump up out of nowhere, half-choking on its chain.

That rabid fury rubbed me the wrong way, repelled me, and I would feel tempted to turn back. It no longer seemed true that there was anyone waiting for me out there.

I felt as though I could sense the presence of what had become universal misery, now that it had reached and tainted even those innocent places, out on the edges of the world.

There would come over me a feeling of bewildered loss which was reflected back to me in everything, and which for that very reason also had, deep down, something sweet to it.

After passing that dilapidated place, I'd walk by another farmhouse that opened out onto the road, and which seemed, as in a fairytale, the good house opposite the wicked house: because it was poor, but happy-looking. Its yard was cluttered with bundles of wood, straw mattresses laid out to dry, long fabrics for swaddling infants: silent but full of life.

Just beyond, there was a wayside shrine; after that, I would make my way directly through the fields, as a shortcut.

XIV

The entrance to the houses was on the other side of a vast marsh in which the path petered out, swallowed up in the darkness of a plane tree and an enormous pine. The flatland then began to slope towards a river, and the paths were sunken and soft. Here and there planks and stones emerged on the stagnant water, put there to facilitate or at least to suggest the way forward. Tetto Murato was made up of a group of houses, little courtyards and gardens, all of it enclosed by four walls.

Through a crumbling arch, one entered into a maze of walls and of roofed structures, of vegetable plots overrun with chickens. The "private abode" that Ada and Paolo shared with the Fantonis was just barely distinguishable from the others, although it was set slightly apart, almost protected by a kind of deserted outdoor atrium, by walls and garden patches which were covered in dirt, buried.

The locals at Tetto Murato—peasant sharecroppers—were poor, slothful and unhealthy; and the houses were the same way. Deep cracks ran through the walls. And yet I felt a secret—even a somewhat distressing—affinity with that desolate place; almost as though it were my true homeland, from which I had once descended. The people who lived there and whom I loved did not like that place, and this too seemed right to me.

I preferred to arrive unseen. I imagined that my nearly daily visits must have seemed extraordinary to the peasants, as if I didn't know that nothing ever amazes them.

Most times I wouldn't see anyone. I would slip through a chipped doorway, go up two flights of steep stone stairs cast in darkness between thick walls. On the landing a small window made the world outside look remote, as if seen in a mirror.

I would push the hefty wood of a small, narrow door. A certain amount of force was needed, but then the door would open with a hollow groan. It was dark on the other side: a heavy curtain, made of blackish-blue velvet, drooped down to the floor (I always forgot to ask, but it must have been from the lost lavish house, rather than from Tetto Murato), hung there by Ada to shield Paolo even more, surrounding him in silence. The act of opening that curtain always seemed like something that wasn't to be taken lightly.

Immediately I would look towards the bed, in the half-light. On one side of the room were two small windows onto the courtyard, windows that only ever let in light through distant reflections, even when the sun was out. On the opposite wall, a window facing the countryside took in the day's final, slanting rays.

My gaze was rarely met with any kind of greeting; Paolo was motionless, but I already knew—by now I knew it too—that he wasn't sleeping.

All the same, I would tiptoe across the room, slowly bringing my feet in their hobnailed shoes to the floor.

As I had seen Ada do, I would lift his hand, let it fall back down: that was how she checked. His hand was inert, unlike the hand of a sleeping person, although not heavy like the rigid hand of a dead man either.

I would take off my fur coat, because a fire was burning in the woodstove; then I'd curl up on the chair next to the bed, prop up my feet and sit there, lost in thought.

Once, while contemplating his hand—so tightly clenched in pain—I knelt down to graze it with my cheek: it was cold. I stood back up, ashamed: I had tasted the audacious, albeit slightly abject, joy of a thief.

I knew for sure that nothing like this would ever have happened in real life. In real life, I hadn't even managed to find out if I was supposed to come to Tetto Murato every day. Sometimes we would just barely greet each other, Paolo and I, and he would apologize for not feeling up to talking. I was sure of only one thing: I was not to ask.

I had tried to get an answer out of Ada: "Should I come?" "He asked you to, but it's up to you. If you can—if it's not too tiring, and if your cousins don't mind." I latched on to that initial take of hers, whereby I had been asked to come once, and once meant for good.

It was nice to sit there, and I found looking at the room pleasant too.

The room didn't feel "remote". It had in it a mix of rustic and refined, of primitive and precious, which for me recalled the flavour of my childhood. The floor of worn, uneven brick, the small windows, and the plaster walls were rough, rustic; but the room was still peppered with signs of a comfortable life, one that might have been, in its own way, just as reserved. There were paintings, coloured prints of the Four Seasons; similar to Melencolias, they were smiling, their oval faces leaning against their round shoulders. Only one of them was laughing: she hid her face behind a furry muff dotted with violets—she must have been Winter.

On the commode, under a bell jar, were wool flowers of a muted, faded colour; and Ada had pointed out to me the tooled-leather bellows, and the green-glass lamp veined with gold. She too liked those objects, of which women are so fond. Paolo, on the other hand, couldn't stand them, was irritated by the mere sight of them. I thought that he saw them as relics of a cloistered and devout world, one he did not love.

There was only one painting that Paolo liked too. It was a fresco painting hanging over the door. Monochrome, nearly erased by humidity, it was just like a chiaroscuro drawing. A solitary shore, a simple house, a tree: it expressed a great peacefulness, a melancholy without end. I would have looked at it always.

Whenever Paolo "woke up", his spirit would suddenly fall back into him, almost violently. He would look bewildered for a second, then say:

"Oh, you're here. I didn't hear you come in."

Paolo didn't realize that he had been "elsewhere" until that moment, and we didn't tell him. I followed Ada's lead in this, as in everything.

"Are you tired?"

"No, walking doesn't tire me. Plus, the way here is beautiful."

Paolo would smile, because the way there was beautiful. He smiled at every expression of enthusiasm, and on top of that he, like Ada, didn't find any beauty in those parts.

Ada had declared that she could only admire famous and spectacular forms of beauty, like the sea, the Matterhorn, and similar sights—and she added that, in her opinion, it was pretentious to consider such humble places more or less beautiful, and even reflected a lack of respect towards them. Paolo didn't comment; doubtless he found Ada's point valid, and in a certain sense even good, ethically speaking. But I thought that he must have been holding on to an ironic dig, which he kept to himself for the time being.

Paolo usually didn't talk much, and his speech was never flashy; but he had many ways of smiling, many subtle shades to his shifting smile.

XV

Sometimes thuds could be heard coming from the stairs, as if a large animal were climbing the steps. There would be the sound of the door banging, then a huffing, while a body just managed to push its way into the room. A young woman appeared, big and blonde; she heaved up her round breasts as she panted, opening her lips to let out a fresh and wild puff of air; clumps of hair fell over her sky-blue eyes; her legs were bare, her socks rolled down. It was Domenica.

Domenica never stayed long: Paolo's presence intimidated her. Whenever Ada sent her into a room where he was, she would say, "The professor's in there." The same way she might have said, "The wolf's in there."

She wasn't actually afraid of men, though: she even, they said, spent time with the farmers at Tetto Murato. Wherever she went, she inspired jealousy in women. She had a husband in prison, and she acted afraid at the thought of him being let out because he used to hit her.

Paolo would struggle to lift his head, searching with his eyes for someone at Domenica's side. Her hand, clenched into a fist, swallowed up the little girl's small hand and most of her forearm.

"Nani!" There was an anxiousness in Paolo's voice whenever he called his daughter's name. And she would look up with her serious face and respond calmly, "Hi, Daddy."

Domenica would ask if she could be of assistance—following instructions left by Ada—and then: "May I go?" And she would run off noisily, pulling Nani along behind her.

Her presence left a sense of cheerfulness, but also embarrassment.

I rarely saw the Fantonis; more often their kids, when they were playing with Nani.

The Fantoni children were beautiful, dressed in fine, vividly coloured clothes. They played "The Prince and the Pauper" alongside the children from Tetto Murato, who had dark clothing and haggard faces. As for Nani, with her hair that glimmered like moon rays, her dark wool clothes made from her father's old coats, she looked like a creature from another world living in exile on the earth.

Their patient games—lining up little pieces of pottery or paper on boards and making believe they were sumptuously laid tables or shop displays—showed that those children, so different in appearance, were really the same and understood one another perfectly.

If it was a sunny day—along the way there, the crowing of roosters from the farmyards seemed a call and response—I would see the children as I neared Tetto Murato, just beyond the shadow of the giant pine tree.

On Thursdays, Ada was there too. She would walk over to meet me with her long, dancelike gait, and I'd hand her the small bouquet I had gathered along the way.

Really, she liked gorgeous flowers, such as roses, but she also made a big to-do over these puny and stunted flowers of late autumn: measly yellow florets, squat daisies, a few pale violets that smelled of nothing.

She admired not the flowers, but the fact that I had picked them. She would say, "Only you, Giulia, know how to make a bouquet this time of year."

Once or twice, Ada succeeded in inviting the Fantonis to come and have tea, with the excuse that they could supply the sugar; she still had not given up on making Paolo—and now me—feel closer to them. Paolo, who was weak in those days, didn't put up a fight.

As for me, either they had changed, or I had changed, because at Tetto Murato the Fantonis no longer bothered me as they had at first.

Signora Fantoni still had a touch of arrogance, but the Major showed discretion and modesty in everything he did, which helped justify Ada's admiration. He wanted to be referred to as a lawyer; it was a joke of Ada's to keep calling him Major. Every time, he gave a slight start and looked around: he considered his situation as an ex-military man risky. And this, in fact, was the very thing Ada found amusing: not that he was scared, but that he believed he was in danger.

The Major asked how long it took me to walk the whole way there, and seemed shocked that I didn't know exactly. His wife also showed an interest in me: she complimented my wool gloves, the cousins' handiwork. Without fail, the Major would ask Paolo about the war. The Major thought highly of Paolo because he was a secondary-school teacher and an intellectual; insofar as he was a partisan, he was mostly a little afraid of him. But clearly he judged that, under the current circumstances, it could do no harm and was even generous for a military man such as himself to consult a "civilian" about the war.

Paolo showed a great deal of patience in answering his questions, never letting on how futile he considered discussing all of it. The Major knew more than he did, in any case, because he listened to the radio broadcasts from London at Signora Sibilla's house; but Paolo helped him, he said, "to get an idea".

XVI

The snow was very late in coming. The weather was cold, though dry and bright, as happens only in places that have no beauty other than the light itself.

Paolo's condition seemed to have left him alone for a period of time; either way, it wasn't something we commented on between us. We never spoke of his malady.

When arriving, I would find Paolo sitting in the sun at the foot of the wall; he would ask to make sure I wasn't tired, and then we'd set out on the roads and the paths. Roads that were just like the ones I took to get to Tetto Murato—grassy, with deep ruts from the wheels of carts. They led over little stone bridges to the scattered farmhouses, passed the small and uneven yards, the black front doors, the stepladders of decrepit wood, and all of them dwindled in the same way into nothing along the gravel bed of a wide and largely dried-up stream.

Paolo liked the gravel bed with its sparse underbrush, and above, the large naked sky; he would sit there for a while, without talking.

We would stop earlier if Paolo was tired, and sit by the side of a ditch on the dry leaves. If he felt like it, we would chat.

The local farmers—one or two passed by, pulling an animal by the halter—seemed unfazed at the sight of city folk: every barn had someone hidden in it, soldier or otherwise. As they walked past us, they would say hello, following old tradition; I noticed that Paolo's way of returning their greeting was courteous, practically ceremonious.

Paolo was never eager to share things that had happened to him recently, but sometimes, in order to illustrate a point, he referenced events from long ago, or memories; and when this happened, his story, though short, would be rich and meaningful like a parable.

And so I learned directly from Paolo different facts about his life and about his childhood: coming from him, they had a calm definitiveness, gave depth and body to the fleeting illuminations offered by Ada.

From these stories, too, I mostly held on to images, though they came to feel like snapshots of stories I had lived firsthand.

His mother, for example (the woman from the painting). Slender, dressed in white, she spent her days dragging herself—in Ada's descriptions—from the bed to the mirror, from the sofa to the piano. Now I knew how hard and strict she had been. One moment stuck with me: Paolo, as a boy, was coming back from a walk in the hills carrying a bunch of wild flowers; she grabbed them out of his hand and threw them to the ground without saying a word.

That sphinx of a mother would then become passionate—yet still cold, incapable of showing affection—whenever Paolo fell ill (and he often did). She would torture herself, making it seem—and maybe, in such moments, it was true—like she did love him, in her own way, with a jealous love. I never found out how much Paolo had suffered from all of this; he talked about it as if he were describing the calmest, most everyday feelings, sometimes even endowing his story with the grave tone of an exemplary tale: something that was perhaps not altogether good, but powerful. And I thought—I was inspired to think—that Paolo truly did not know resentment; or that he had a deeper knowledge of human affection, which went much further than I could imagine.

In any case, my initial impression had, for me, been confirmed: that Paolo's true mother was Ada.

When it was time for me to head off, Paolo would wrap himself in his large black cloak—the air was very cold by that point—and walk with me up to where the path met the country road.

As we neared the road, we would see Ada pop up in the distance on her bicycle: she didn't take my shortcut, which was hard to cycle along. She would also spot us from afar, and wave; and she would hop off her bicycle with her somewhat brusque gracefulness. She wore a tight-fitting jacket with vivid stripes, in which yellow stood out the most: a jacket for summer evenings. She often adorned the handlebars with vegetables, green trophies. She was pleased with her acquisitions, which guaranteed food for a few days, and she invited me to stay for dinner and to sleep at Tetto Murato. I hesitated; I was never in high spirits at that time of evening, and felt uncertain. I told her that I couldn't possibly announce this other novelty to the cousins.

"But isn't it strange," she'd say, "for you to travel so far every day, and then you're not brave enough to say you're staying over for just one night?"

"Some other time." And with the matter settled, I'd set out on my way.

If I turned around, I'd still see them on the path beneath the large trees, "figures moving away in a tapestry".

I'd keep going on the road, under the great cold sky, in which the rayless moon shone, solitary and precious.

While walking, I felt tired, homesick: not for the cousins' home. Later, in the cold room, in the uncomfortable bed, I'd hug the hot-water bottle.

XVII

It was strange that the cousins never tried to find out anything about Paolo's illness. If I thought of how they cared in particular about the sick, how eager they always were to help—through prayer—and, also, how much they liked to talk, a little pedantically, about illnesses, it was strange that they had never asked me any questions; or rather, since they weren't the sort of women to ask questions, that they hadn't pressed me for any news. The truth was, from the outset I had hoped to get on their good side and even to win them over with this.

There had been another part to the story too. Ada had told me to inform the cousins that on certain days a backstreet butcher was open in the countryside; if they wanted, she could buy things for them. I had casually thrown out the offer, expecting one of their usual polite-distrustful refusals (and hoping for just that, considering the trouble of having to carry the meat and pass the checkpoint with a large parcel). Instead, they expressed their thanks and accepted. The whole thing meant a lot to Ada. If she couldn't run there herself, she gave Domenica countless instructions, and when they divided up what had been purchased, she chose the best pieces for the cousins.

They knitted a pair of wool gloves for Nani, endlessly appreciated by Ada, and for which she thanked them with a note, written in her rapid and hyperbolic style.

But that's where things ended between them.

What's more, I was always good to the cousins. I read aloud to them in the evening and if they proposed, shyly (fearing rejection), that we recite the rosary together, I'd accept. But I never spoke about Ada and Paolo with them: I sensed disapproval in their silence.

XVIII

Maybe, in the end, it was the snow.

The old road seemed to blur into its surroundings, then start again, go on without end. Yet the veil of snow wasn't thick, only a sprinkling of white in the nightlike winter afternoon: a cloud that one second was whirling and the next had slowed, as though unsure whether to settle on the ground or disappear.

I was tired when I arrived at Tetto Murato, and later, when it was time for me to get ready to leave, I could feel my head beginning to spin at the sight of the completely white landscape, the untrodden road.

"You absolutely cannot go," Ada said.

I felt a tangled knot come undone in me. I said okay.

At Tetto Murato, dinner was served by the glow of an acetylene lamp in the big rustic kitchen, the walls sinking into the darkness like in a grotto.

Everyone sat around a long table full of life. There were the two families with their children, and the two maids.

Domenica was big in the shadows and, if she appeared in the light, resplendent like an allegorical portrait of Summer;

meanwhile the other girl, Bruna, who worked for the Fantonis, was pale and inscrutable. Younger than Domenica to whom she was a friend-enemy, Bruna was honest, and had a boyfriend in the mountains; whereas Domenica, they said, was capable of going up in the hayloft with just about anybody. Seeing the way Domenica stared out of two eyes as unclouded as the sky, you could tell that everything near her came to reflect a natural simplicity. The prudish Fantonis regarded her with apprehension: they considered it one of Paolo and Ada's many peculiarities, or even worse, one of their imprudent missteps, keeping a woman like that in their house.

The children, and not just Nani, but also the Fantoni children who were more obviously from the city, adored Domenica. They would jump all over her, touch her, squeeze her, jitter to the sound of her shouting, her laughter, excited and happy. Bruna knew how to play better, she knew real games, but she wasn't always in the mood; and besides, Domenica was the only one who never ratted them out for anything. Domenica was like a bed to jump on, a field for doing somersaults. Once Pietruccio, the Fantonis' son, contemplating Domenica, had thrown open his arms as if he had just had a revelation:

"Domenica is as nice and big as a church dome!"

Ada was proud of the dinner and therefore happy that I had decided to stay over that night.

The two families shared their meals, made by Ada and Signora Fantoni on alternating days. Ada had managed to get her hands on butter and had boiled potatoes. The block of butter was placed whole in the middle of the table; once spread on the yellow pulp of the potatoes, its milky whiteness softened and melted.

Heat emanated from the iron kitchen stove, which was lit only for lunch and dinner, and everyone had flushed faces.

The two couples sat across from each other: between Ada and Paolo was Nani, while the Fantonis kept their youngest son in the middle and their two older children at their sides: snooty Anna Laura, with her long eyelashes, and frenetic Pietruccio.

The youngest, who hadn't started talking yet, was hitting his spoon against the table.

I felt happy, and at the same time melancholy, as if the current joy were the resurfacing of another, forgotten happiness.

Where, then, had there already been that cheerful table full of people, that dark kitchen, the curt voices of the maids, the high-pitched voices of the children, and the slow voice, like a lullaby, of the woman sitting in front of me?

My mind drifted for a moment in a game, trying to trace the different shades of light. The acetylene flame, Nani's hair shimmering like a second light on her forehead, the toddler's face. But nicer still were the shades of white in the shadows: the maids' aprons, the dishes in the cupboard, and then all the way in the dark corner by the kitchen sink and through the low window, as if coming from the beyond, the faint glimmer of snow.

Once the stove had been turned off, shudders and puffs of freezing air started to whisk their way around the room. The Major, holding the lamp and carrying his son on his shoulders, was the first to face the dark and cold of the stairs, followed by his wife, who was leading their other children by the hand.

Nani, her hand already clasped in Domenica's fist, was waiting, seemingly guarded by the woman's oddly maternal smile, which I had never seen on her before. Nani slept with Domenica in the dining room on the ground floor. Looking at them together, it was apparent that a kind of harmony had taken shape between them: the girl, just a little thing, seemed almost an offshoot of that female giant, whose unrefined beauty had in turn been rendered kind, almost pensive, by her duty as protectress. I lightly touched Nani's hair, without even trying to kiss her on the cheek. Ada and Paolo never kissed her; they enveloped her in unchanging tenderness, but they didn't coddle her. (Whereas it was curious to hear the Fantonis sharply address their children as "sweetheart", "sweetie", or even "little saint".)

We all said goodnight on the landing.

Signora Fantoni asked, "Where are you going to have Giulia sleep?"

Ada already had an answer prepared. "On the sofa, where Alessandra used to sleep."

"But it's so small," she pointed out.

"Giulia isn't fussy," Ada replied. The Major seemed embarrassed; Paolo and I were waiting like children when the adults make arrangements for where they'll go without consulting them. (As for Alessandra, that was Nani's real name: Ada regretted that it had been replaced by that nickname, and she promised herself she would go back to using it.)

It was clear that Ada had something in mind, an idea that hadn't been premeditated—she resolved every issue as it arose— though it became incontestable from the moment she'd had it.

As soon as we were alone, she said, "We could squeeze a bit and make room for Giulia next to us."

"But will she want that?" Paolo asked.

"It's no problem for me."

"If it turns out to be uncomfortable, I'll sleep on the floor," Paolo added.

"No one's sleeping on the floor," Ada declared. "We don't have any extra blankets."

Ada gave me a nightgown. She pulled it out from a drawer in the dresser, unfolded it for me to see: it was made of voile and lace, and had an elaborately refined style. She showed me the other nightgowns in the drawer: they were similar to the first one, transparent, low-cut, frilly. She pointed out that some of what looked like openwork had actually been the wear of time. The nightgowns had belonged to Paolo's mother.

Ada put on one that was sky-blue. From her collar and sleeves poked out her long-sleeved wool shirt, which, grey and thick, was actually for a man; and she looked just like those peasant children dressed up as angels in processions, who wear baby-blue tunics over their dark clothes.

Since I didn't have a shirt on underneath, I slipped a sweater on over the voile nightgown, and took my spot in the bed after Ada, who had lain down in the middle. The bed was quite wide.

While we were rummaging through the nightgowns, Paolo had got undressed; now he was lying down facing the wall.

The acetylene flame was flickering out, placed outside the door so the room wouldn't smell. There was nothing in the dark but a red glimmer at the bottom of the woodstove.

"How nice to have Giulia here," Ada sighed; then she curled up, said, "Goodnight," and she was already asleep.

A single fur blanket was spread on top of the bed. Soft, warm and light (another relic of old wealth), it had a fabulous name: vicuna.

The stove at the foot of the bed emitted heat, but the siege of the night and the cold was pressing up against the small windows. I lay motionless, the fur weighing lightly and pleasantly on my body, in the warmth and in the faint scent of that bed that wasn't my own. "Their" bed. I was a bit perturbed, but happy, too. It had been easy: with Ada, everything was easy.

I must have dozed off with these thoughts in my head, because they were still there when something woke me.

Ada had sat up in the bed and was calling out, "Paolo!"

I could feel her climb over his body, saw her strike a match with trembling hands.

I was ashamed to be there, I felt like I was in the way, an intruder. Ada raised the light over Paolo. Paolo, propped up on his side, was pressing both hands against his heart.

"Camphor!" Ada said. Without putting down the lamp, she grabbed her robe off its nail, and moving the lamp from one hand to the other, slipped it on and was about to run off (to call for the Major, I'd find out later). But then she stopped and stood there suspended, seemingly frozen mid-sprint, struck by a sudden thought. Breathing heavily, she turned towards Paolo, then without saying anything, besides a "Sorry" directed at me, she lifted the curtain and was gone.

It took time to boil the needle, and first the stove had to be lit with twigs and brushwood in the freezing kitchen. (She told me, afterwards, how mean things and objects seemed in those moments as they all but fought against her.)

I waited in a state of shock; but Ada's concern for me had also granted a sense of security, of tenderness.

When Ada, without making a sound, reappeared—pushing aside the curtain with her elbow, the lamp in one hand and the saucepan with the syringe in the other—I jumped out of the bed and went over to her; she handed me the lamp and quickly began to prepare everything.

When she approached Paolo, holding the loaded syringe high in the air, he stared up at her with an interrogative, frightened expression.

She said, "I'll be able to do it. You'll see."

Exhausted, Paolo gave in and closed his eyes. Ada abruptly flung off the covers, furrowed her brow, planted the needle with excessive energy. "For his heart," she said to me. But she went on staring at Paolo sullenly, until she could finally say: "There, he's better now."

Paolo's breathing was becoming more relaxed. Ada slipped back into bed next to him, on the side near the wall. "It will be easier if I need to get up again," she said. She had just enough time to add "Goodnight," and she had fallen back asleep.

Lying with my eyes opened wide in the dark, I listened to her breathing, which was so different when she slept. I couldn't make out Paolo's. Instead I heard, a little later, his voice calling out to me softly.

"Giulia."

"Yes."

"You're not tired?"

"No."

"Were you scared?"

"A bit," I replied, and a wave of warmth flooded through me; with Ada far away in sleep, I had started to feel alone.

"I was scared too, when I saw Ada with the needle. I couldn't understand."

"Did it hurt a lot?"

"Not that much. It was the first time, you know? I've always had the injections from the Major. He's the only one around here who knows how. Ada must have thought that she couldn't call for him, this time."

I saw again Ada's face in the lamplight, perplexed, wide-eyed, her quick glance in which flickered, even in that anxious moment, a hint of laughter.

"She doesn't want to upset the Fantonis, doesn't want to offend them. But most of all she didn't want them to think badly of you."

I opened my eyes to the snow's milky light coming in through the small windows, and saw, as though my vision from the night before were repeating itself, Ada pushing open the curtain with her elbow. This time she wasn't holding the lamp but a basket tray, with tea and slices of toasted bread (Paolo called it scorched bread).

Ada declared, "All's well!"

She offered Paolo tea, which he turned down since it wasn't sweetened. I nibbled on the bread, liking its bitter burnt taste.

Ada slipped off her robe, got back into bed, and rested the tray on her knees; she ate her bread for a while, taking little sips of her tea, defying Paolo's teasing with a sense of gratitude for the things that supported her. She started filling us in: she had instructed Domenica not to bring Nani up to say good morning until she had gone back down and everything was in order.

"What's that supposed to mean?" Paolo asked.

"I'll make the bed; that way it can seem like Giulia slept on the floor. The only one who comes in here is Domenica."

Paolo looked sceptical. I didn't feel embarrassed, but calm, completely under Ada's protection. She had explained things, she said, to the Fantonis; the wife had been the one to bring it up.

"Last night I could have sworn I heard you."

"Sure, you know how his heart gets. Last night was a bad one."

"And you didn't call Federico? Didn't he need a shot?"

"I did it."

"You?"

As Ada told us this I was already thinking, without even knowing why, that I had to leave—and while it was so nice to stay. Maybe it was a fear that I could ruin, by pushing further, the joy I had felt; most of all, it was the need to contemplate, to fully savour that gift, like a child who chooses to go and play all alone with a new present.

"I need to go now," I said.

Surprised, Ada stopped for a second to think of any arguments she could make against my decision, and she tried out a few, until, as usual, her fear of insisting, of forcing others, won out.

"If you've made up your mind, so be it."

I was annoyed with myself for running off, and yet it felt good to wind up on my own again—just myself and the road.

The road was stretched out like a dead man under the snow. And all around was a sense of amazement and, along with it, gratification, the kind felt by someone who has received an answer, the kind that rests on the face of the dead. The sky, still heavy with imminent snow, met the earth's purity like murky chaos, negation, nothingness.

When I was on the bridge, and the town appeared black and white before me, I realized that another reason I had left so quickly was my concern that the cousins were worried about me. I knew that the whole thing must have been almost inconceivable to them.

XIX

Now that the piazza had become a snowy desert, on market days the stalls were lined up under the porticoes, turning them into crammed corridors or lanes swept by gusts of freezing air.

The market run by the farmers, once as merry as a fair, had been reduced to an offering of raw and oily brown wool and a few outdated, handcrafted agrarian tools.

I walked along, tossed about by the small crowd of locals who moved blindly like herds, eyes fixed and a bit dazed. A crowd made up of old people and women: younger men couldn't risk coming down into town, since a few days earlier, "Muti's men" had torn up the papers of a couple of dozen and then deported them.

I stalled among the slow shoves of the crowd as between the slow-moving flanks of cattle, in front of a stand displaying combs, compact mirrors, inexpensive necklaces.

I picked out a brooch shaped like a squirrel, pinned onto a thin piece of cardboard. They wrapped it for me in a piece of rumpled blue paper.

I pushed the wrapped pin down to the bottom of my coat pocket. The lining inside the pocket frequently came unstitched:

as I walked, I checked multiple times with my hand that the gift was still there.

Once I arrived, while kicking my feet against a step to remove the snow, I took out the blue wrapping: it was empty, closed and flat like the shell of a dead insect. I stood there dismayed, but only for a second—the lining inside the pocket, which was uneven from all the times it had been resewn, had little cavities into which the squirrel had burrowed.

Nani was in the kitchen, sitting on her little stool by Domenica's feet. Domenica was making dough for gnocchi, had mixed the potatoes and flour and was giving big whacks to the kneading tray. Now and then she tossed pieces of potato—the hardest ones which she couldn't knead—into Nani's lap, as if to a dog. Nani took them between two fingers and chewed on them methodically, her lips shut, her small body upright, in her usual dignified manner.

She blushed with joy as she took the brooch and showed it to Domenica, who then examined it, pursing her lips admiringly and giving vigorous nods of the head.

"How is he?" I asked her.

Domenica's face expressed confusion, then concentration as intense as it was useless. "I have no idea," she said finally.

Upstairs, I found Ada, who was wearing her "mean" face.

She had her back to the woodstove: it was the pose she often assumed when standing still. She warmed her back like this, and always ended up singeing her clothes, a fact that accentuated her peculiar air between aristocrat and gipsy, especially when she wore her orange voile robe lined with black velvet (an item inherited from Paolo's mother). Paolo, who couldn't stand untidiness, was always exhorting her—even during his episodes, through gestures—to move away from the fire.

Frowning, Ada was looking down at the floor so as to stand her ground; because Paolo, while slamming his head down onto the pillow, was groaning, "Ada, I'm begging you." He now felt spasms of pain in his head, which made him gnash his teeth.

"We already did three today," Ada said sullenly. She was referring to the injections. "I'm not giving you a fourth."

"You're right," Paolo groaned; then he started appealing to her again: "Ada!"

I felt sorry for him, was nearly in pain myself just watching him. Ada seemed harsh to me. And yet, at the same time, I couldn't help but admire how there was almost an art to Paolo's tortured expression, an art whose aim was to mesmerize Ada.

When Paolo's groaning had ceased, but his breaths had begun to come out choked by the onset of an asthma attack, Ada's expression suddenly changed—from resistant to anxious, heedful. "Just a second!" she said, and feverishly set about preparing everything.

After the injection, Paolo became calm and started to doze off. Ada said to me:

"Please, spend the night here. Stay with me."

With me: so then, Ada, too, could feel loneliness? I said yes, I would stay, and in the meantime I looked at her, perhaps searching for confirmation that I had understood correctly. But she was already making herself busy, closing the shutters, smiling; she had gone back to being light and active.

There was a soft knock at the door. It was Nani; she tiptoed into the room, as quiet as a mouse, directing her light-coloured, practically white eyes at "Signora Giulia" with shy complicity. She walked over to the bed to let her daddy take a good look at how pretty she was.

Paolo opened his eyes and noticed the new piece of jewellery on her sweater.

"It's beautiful on you, Nani. But who in the world gave it to you?"

"Signora Giulia," Nani replied, with her typical seriousness.

"You know, it's really beautiful, Nani."

"She'll end up being a bit shallow like me," Ada remarked conclusively.

XX

Ada and I were heading upstairs after finishing dinner. Paolo hadn't come down to eat. Halfway up the stairs, Ada grabbed my hand and squeezed it convulsively, standing still to listen.

I heard, discordant but sweet, the hum of faint voices—the children saying their prayers—but right after, in the stairs' crypt-like silence, there was also a grating sound, like something being filed down. And in the dark bedroom, while Ada lit the oil lamp with feverish hands, that asthmatic rattle became frightening, similar to the growl of a wild animal.

Now Paolo was lying in tensed agony, waiting for his breath to return. Like a fighter he arched his body to brace himself, wriggled free. It was a show of strength, a battle in which only one of the adversaries was visible.

The Major, having tiptoed in, was probing the situation with his kind and round eyes, which were full of fear, or perhaps only surprise.

Paolo, rendered mute by his asthma, seemed oddly expressive, desperate to persuade, like someone gagged and bound who wants to convince the others of some danger they don't see, of the urgent need to be afraid and to flee—while they, unable to understand, remain equally mute and motionless.

But Paolo's eye—the look buried deep in his eyes—was still averse to any kind of entreaty, only distant and sad.

These moments of tension, while we waited for his breath to push its way through, became unbearable. Ada and I were twisting our hands in knots; the Major counted on his wristwatch the seconds as they passed.

All of a sudden, without even changing expression—only his dishevelled mane gave him a bit of a wild air—Paolo abruptly threw off the blankets, pulled off his pajama top and his wool undershirt, and in two hops was at the window, flinging it open and trying to find some air.

Ada was quick to act: she—with the Major's help—threw the fur blanket onto him. Paolo collapsed into a chair; he looked around, disoriented yet grandiose (like a mad old king) while his uneven, laboured breath eased back into his exhausted chest.

The Major, who had timed everything, perked up, commenting on the attack's record time. Even though she knew he had good intentions, that apparent technical interest of his, that sports fan's enthusiasm, seemed hilarious to Ada who, still wired after all the tension, had turned cheerful (as they say happens in battle, between rounds of fire).

"So you've enjoyed yourselves?" Paolo said in a whisper as he saw her laughing, though already he was looking to join in the joke.

"You put on quite the show," Ada said. "I'd say Giulia won't have any reason to regret staying over." And meanwhile she caressed him with her big and long maternal hands, tidying his messy hair. But Paolo wasn't wild about being touched, not even by her, and he had her give him a comb.

"Good thing you can at least have fun at my expense," he said, and I could see that he was relieved, serene.

"But you did give us a scare—when you opened the window."

"Were you afraid I wanted to jump?"

"I was afraid you'd catch pneumonia."

There was a sound: a thumping knock at the door. "Domenica?" It had to be her.

"Nani is scared of dying," Domenica announced, not with her characteristic alarmist tone, with which she would have stated that the stove wasn't lighting, but placidly, as though it were obvious.

"I'm coming," Ada replied with the same tone of voice, though she did heave a sigh, as if to say: that's all we needed now.

Paolo, as he often did when Domenica entered the room, had closed his eyes. He opened them when we were alone, and smiled at me.

"Come to bed in the meantime," and he closed his eyes again.

I took one of the fanciful nightgowns from the drawer, got undressed quickly, and sat down on the bed. Paolo was quiet. The curtain opened and Ada shouted as she walked in:

"Giulia, you have no idea how good that looks on you. You're breathtaking."

Paolo came back to life with a start. He didn't look at me, but at Ada: she could still surprise him.

"Come, look at yourself in the mirror." Ada took me by

the hand, led me in front of the mirror resting on top of the commode, and raised the light in her hand up to my face. Our images emerged on the surface of the old, murky mirror, vague and enchanted like in the water of a pond.

"What about Nani?" Paolo asked.

"The usual. She was afraid she'd die."

"Has she calmed down now?"

"Oh yes."

"But how do you manage to console her?" I asked.

"I promise her that she won't die tonight."

"And what does she say to that?"

"She makes me repeat it a thousand times. Then when it seems like she has already relaxed and I'm about to go, she calls me back and says slowly, emphasizing each word the way she does: 'But-I'm-still, still-afraid-of-dying.'"

"She shouldn't stay downstairs," Paolo said, concerned.

"She's perfectly fine downstairs. She was afraid of dying when she slept in here, too. Dying—her! How silly."

And Ada laughed. I thought that in this case—and it was all for the best—Ada was truly lacking in imagination.

Ada took her spot in the bed. Paolo asked her pleadingly, "Couldn't we leave the light on just for a little while?"

"There's probably not much oil left. But it doesn't matter, we'll find some more."

"Okay, put it out then," Paolo sighed.

"No, no. I'll get the Fantonis to give me some."

"You know perfectly well they won't. Besides, I don't think they have any extra either."

"They do, I'm sure they do. And if they don't give it to me, I'll take just a little."

I didn't say anything, only looked at her, stunned.

"You didn't think I would?" Ada said.

"In town people point you out, even fear you, for being two raging moralists."

"Ah well," Ada said joyfully, "you have to watch out for moralists."

Paolo laughed in his unique, noiseless way. He asked, "What about bread? Do we have any?"

"Now bread I'm always good for," Ada exclaimed triumphantly. "Are you hungry?"

"Would it seem all that unreasonable to you?"

"I'll run and get some."

A moment later and she was back.

"I brought you cheese, too."

"The Fantonis' cheese?"

"No, no. It's ours."

"Nani?"

"She was sleeping. I kissed her on her head. I have to wash her hair: it smells like a barn."

Ada had slipped in under the covers while she spoke and, like someone concluding a day that has been full and intense but also good, said with one of her long, sweet exhalations: "How lovely. Everything is okay. Nani is sleeping, Paolo is eating, Giulia is here with us. The war will end and we'll go back home. Paolo will be well, he'll be important. Will I have a dress made for when you go to the Constituent Assembly, Paolo?"

Paolo smiled—winking—at me. He asked, "There weren't any pears?"

"Oh yes, those 'good and ugly' ones. There's a whole basket. But it's up there," and Ada pointed to the mystery of shadows above the wardrobe. "The basket's all the way up on the top."

In her angel's tunic, Ada seemed to want to take off, to fly towards the ceiling. She fell back down to the ground. Paolo laughed. "You see, Ada, you're beautiful, but I'm afraid you don't know how to fly."

"Can I try?" I wasn't taller than Ada, but I was better at climbing. I got up on a chair placed on a small table, and threw my arms around the basket.

We grabbed the pears, happy as kids who had just stolen them. Ada and I bit into ours right away; Paolo—if as a child he had ever been lured into stealing pears, which was unlikely, he had almost certainly done the same thing then, too—insisted on using a penknife, peeling the pear and cutting it into bite-size pieces.

Having finished gnawing on hers, Ada lifted her regal profile to take aim, and with a rapid flick of the arm threw the core into the corner.

"Damn!" I said.

"Oh yes," Ada replied, "you've got plenty to be scandalized over."

Paolo looked back and forth at the two of us with gleeful eyes.

Ada heaved a sigh to herself, though sweetly, sleepily. She asked, "Can I put it out?" then blew on the waning flame.

In that moment there was an explosion in the room: comical and festive, like in a game. We saw the iron lid shoot up from the stove in a halo of sparks and then fall back down with a funny thud, followed by a kind of whimper.

We burst out laughing. Each one of us laughed the way he or she must have laughed as a child, Paolo making with quick hiccups his noiseless chuckle; Ada pleasantly, relaxed, as if she were singing, as if she were already dreaming; me trying to hold back with stifled silences my rather unrestrained laugh.

Later, in the warmth of the thick and light fur blanket—though cold air brushed against our faces as if the old walls couldn't protect us from the chill of the snow-covered countryside, while the fire, now close to dying and shivering as if in agony, was only as warm as a large animal curled up in the middle of the room—I lay thinking.

Ada had evoked a happy future. Well, no matter how things went, should even the opposite come to pass, with Paolo not at all important, but ever more solitary and reserved, or even still sick, and the two of them still without any money, one thing was certain: in spite of everything, Ada would, in fact, be happy. Even if she were tired and couldn't take any more, even if she felt disillusioned, as in stripped of all illusions. Happy about the fact that she was useful, in that moment—she and not someone else—to Paolo and Nani.

But in relaxed moments, free of anxiety and open to dreams, would she recall the pain, the stories from another time, or would she always go on dreaming, as she did now, of the future?

I thought all of this, and I feared I was destined to disappear for Ada when the course of events eventually separated us. Didn't she herself often say that when Nani grew up she should feel free to go out into the world to learn, or to get married? So, to Nani, as well, she was attached only for the amount of time the girl needed her. And so I feared that in forgetting, as she would, Tetto Murato, Ada would have me to forget too.

XXI

When I awoke, the sun was out. Ada was washing herself. She had thrown open the shutters, and the white sun came in from the side facing the yard; through the western window, which looked out onto the countryside, I could see the mountains glimmering. The room, besides a streak of white light, remained grey, almost dark throughout.

Ada was next to the washing basin, placed on an iron trivet, and at her feet was the jug of hot water which Domenica had left outside the door as per instructions. She had taken off her nightgown, and she had on only her famous man's shirt, its long sleeves rolled up to her elbows.

I saw her, from behind, then in profile, as she bent over the basin and stood back up: her chest, inside the thick shirt, was slender and flat as a boy's, and the outline of her naked body underneath drew curves which, while soft, were clean, like the lean body of an adolescent.

"Paolo, look—Ada looks like a Manzù drawing."

Paolo didn't respond, but turned up his nose: he couldn't stand "Catholic" modern artists.

Now Ada was about to open the window. Paolo shouted, "Ada! Don't let them see you like that!"

"Sure, sure," she said, and meanwhile, with rapid movements, she flung open the window onto the yard—the small inner courtyard surrounded by blind walls, now full of snow—and having grabbed the basin with two hands, threw the soapy water into the air.

"Did you at least check to see that no one was there?"

It wasn't dumping the water out the window that was strange; it was, rather, doing it at Tetto Murato.

"Everything's fine," Ada said as she got dressed quickly, a bit haphazardly, already anxious to run downstairs.

"You see? She doesn't pay any mind to these things, but the locals don't joke around. You can guess for yourself whether she's looking to offend them; only that when something's natural to her, in her head it seems impossible for someone else to find it scandalous. But she found out as much when she gave Nani a bath in the yard. It was around when she had first come here. She'd taken the tub outside to wash the girl in the sun. I don't think they even saw her; it must have been their children who told them. Later, they said to Nani: 'Your mamma's the Devil.'"

I knew that Ada was friends, in her own way, with the local peasants at Tetto Murato. She brought them medicine for free: quinine, aspirin, cough syrup; they welcomed her and always treated her well, aside from when she bought spinach and they made her pay double what it cost in town.

Once I had stumbled upon Ada talking to a countrywoman sitting in front of the houses. A woman who seemed old but was young—coarse, pale, dressed in black. They were laughing together. Ada with her radiant laugh, the woman already missing teeth, her large belly bouncing, her dark eyes concealed under a black headscarf lowered to block out the sunlight. Ada was standing up, erect, as was natural for her, not in the condescending way of "proper ladies", but simply as though the two of them were the same—certain, rather than hopeful, that they were the same.

Paolo, on the other hand, intimidated the locals, maybe because he was too nice, maybe because to engage them, he asked questions they didn't understand. They scratched their heads under their hats in embarrassment, looked at the weather—that is, the sky—and simply couldn't talk to him.

Only a young man, who was in hiding and living in the barn, used to have conversations with Paolo while sitting out in the sun. The word around Tetto Murato was that he was Domenica's lover, and that he ate his bread free of charge. He had come from a place where words came more easily to people. (One day he simply vanished, and we found out that he had taken Paolo's bicycle with him.)

XXII

Paolo was uneasy, especially on days when his attacks were less frequent and less intense. Coming into the bedroom, I wasn't even sure if he was glad to see me: his greeting seemed cold.

Ada—the schools were closed—was always at Tetto Murato now. Taking advantage of when Paolo seemed to doze off, she would quietly start to dust the room, something she could never manage to do at the right time. Paolo, as if spying on her from behind his eyelashes, would immediately protest:

"Please, Ada, don't start pacing around the place now."

"I'll stop in a second. I'm just going to sweep up a little dust."

"Not now, please."

Then she would stop, letting out a sigh.

Or Ada would announce that she had to go downstairs.

"I'll just be a moment. I need to teach Luisa a knitting stitch."

"She can teach you as many as you could dream of. Besides, why in the world do you need to teach it to her now?"

"Right—really there's no need to teach it to her now. But anyway, I should go downstairs to tell Domenica to put the apples in the oven."

"Can't she come upstairs to take orders?"

"Sure, she can come up. Tomorrow I'll tell her to come up."

Ada already seemed slightly angry, but deep down she must have liked these skirmishes. I, on the other hand, felt uncomfortable. "I'll go downstairs to tell her," I offered.

And Paolo: "Is it absolutely necessary that we eat baked apples?"

"No, it's not necessary—we can eat them raw, too."

She had spoken curtly: now she was being her mean self (for fun). And that was as far as her anger went.

Once, walking into the room, I noticed that the bell jar with the wool flowers was no longer in a corner on top of the wardrobe, where it had been banished because Paolo couldn't stand the sight of it.

Ada gestured with her hands, as if to say, "it's gone," and she threw a glance at Paolo to check that he wouldn't be bothered hearing her talk about it.

She told me quickly, under her breath. It had happened during one of his attacks. Paolo had suddenly jumped up from the bed, furious as a boy starting a fistfight with a classmate, had grabbed the bell with both hands and thrown it to the ground. Afterwards, he didn't show any sign of noticing that the bell jar had disappeared, as though he already knew; yet Ada was sure that he hadn't been "awake" in that moment, specifically because he had done what he never would have done in a conscious state—destroying an object that didn't belong to him in order be rid of an annoyance.

"We'll reimburse the owner for this too when the war's over," Ada resolved.

Whether sick or not, Paolo was certainly the most consistent person in terms of who he was, and his physiognomy the least prone to variation, besides when making a tired or wry expression; nor could any emotion or passion show itself in any other way. One time, Paolo's face altered, the way an actor's face might. It hadn't fully changed, really, but it looked deformed, almost as though he were making a caricature of himself, and it had an immodest touch to it, like the face of someone aroused by wine. His voice was the first thing he changed: he made it sound round and eloquent, and he was speaking French, courting a woman.

The two of us—Ada and I—almost choked trying to hold back our laughter, not wanting to miss a word; we didn't even have time to express to each other our surprise and our amusement.

The tone was that of a chivalrous, burlesque comedy, with risqué references but literary jargon, too: strange as this was, it still might not have been much on its own, but it soon became clear that the woman Paolo was speaking to, whom he called *Louise*, was none other than Luisa Fantoni.

Signora Fantoni was pretty, but the compliments being directed at her by her suitor (it was impossible to think: Paolo) with the clear aim of teasing her only brought to mind her flaws, which were minimal in a good-looking person, yet enough to leave her with little allure. He lauded her thin ankles and you couldn't help but think they were actually a bit thick, praised her *souplesse* and you were reminded of her weight.

The game didn't last long; Paolo seemed to give in to fatigue and boredom, his face suddenly going back to how it always was, impenetrable and sad.

Ada and I couldn't stop referencing the scene when it was over, letting ourselves go in unrestrained laughter.

"Are you laughing at me?" Paolo asked.

The next day, Signora Fantoni said, "Yesterday, I could have sworn I heard you two laughing."

"Sure did," Ada replied. "It was one of the most entertaining performances Paolo has given us thus far."

I observed Signora Fantoni's face, and I was unable to understand how she could continue to treat Ada with condescension and not be, on the contrary, slightly afraid of her.

XXIII

"I should go to take the Coramine back to Sibilla," Ada
announced.

And Paolo: "Right now?"

"I'll go," I ventured.

"Can I go too?" Nani asked calmly, though with unexpected
firmness.

We all laughed at Nani's nerve, and Ada explained that
Signora Sibilla had a cat, strange like everything of Signora
Sibilla's, which let Nani pet it.

Rather than cut across the farmyards, I chose to go around
Tetto Murato, even though it took longer, for fear of running
into unfamiliar dogs. The way was just barely marked: it wasn't
a very cold evening, and the snow had started to melt a little.
After skirting the outer wall of Tetto Murato, the path ended at
a road reduced to a simple trail in the snow; it continued after
a curve, running along a high wall behind which loomed the
trees of a deserted park, before leading to the farmyards of Tetti
Gallo. I had gone, as a child with the cousins, to see Signora
Sibilla one summer afternoon; I remembered the garden, but

not the farmhouse, which either way was unrecognizable on a winter evening.

Here too, as at Tetto Murato, the old property had been divided—Sibilla herself owned just a few acres at this point—and neglect and destitution had left everything to decay. Also here the road, after reaching the houses, sank down into a perpetual marsh, currently of melted snow.

I had to pick up the girl and carry her: such a tender little thing, it seemed strange that she weighed so much.

Suddenly, I found myself surrounded by terrors that I had deluded myself into thinking I had lost over time. A black dog appeared with its tail between its legs just a few steps away, light as a shadow; he was growling softly, with a rage that didn't seem to fit an animal so much as a human.

It was almost a relief for me to feel the girl's heart beating, and then the barking of other dogs. But these dogs soon appeared, howling, and they looked like wolves. It dawned on me that the farmers who lived there might be expecting the Germans and therefore would not come out; it also occurred to me that Signora Sibilla lived alone and maybe wouldn't open up either.

But a tall man carrying a dark lantern was there, and raising his lantern he showed me the gate to the garden just behind him; then he opened it with a large key and gave a tug at an iron wire, which must have connected to a bell inside the house; he led me across the garden buried in snow, knocked at a door, turned the doorknob.

"She's in the greenhouse," he said in a grave, prayerful voice. "She's able to keep warm in there."

Enormous, wrapped in two or three layers, Signora Sibilla was sitting in a room that creepers and vines had turned into a cave.

"The woodstove is for both the plants and me," she said.

Sibilla's face was big too, magisterial like the face of an ancient statue or painting.

She had been a beautiful woman, and had received her fair share of criticism back in that provincial town; now she was old, almost poor, and no stranger to sorrow: they said that a daughter of hers had killed herself. She still seemed full of life in her dark eyes under imperious eyebrows, whereas I had suspected that she had changed, softened, given that—going by what the Fantonis said—she got along so well with that couple. But there she was, the same woman as ever. She was feared, in town, for her judgements, a form of payback for the disapproval she'd received long ago. Precisely because she could be so harsh, her friendliness had a real, perhaps teasing but never duplicitous, flavour to it.

Referencing the cousins, she said, "Poor gals! They never got married so that they'd never be wrong about anything," and she smiled, a bit mysteriously.

"They gave you the room? What good gals. It's true, though, that otherwise the authorities would have requisitioned it." Then she laughed at my astonishment.

"And what about this pretty little lady?"

Nani was looking spellbound at the cat lying in its owner's lap. She cautiously reached out a hand, but this time her shy caress was unwelcome. The cat jumped down and started to strut around between the potted plants with an air of self-importance. Clearly it was unaware of its own repugnant appearance, otherwise it wouldn't have been so proud: it was speckled, or rather chequered, with patches of missing fur. Sibilla explained that she had been the one to shave it like that, because, she said, with its fur less tempting, they would be less likely to kill it.

She gave a few sugar cubes to Nani and asked me in dialect how her dad was doing.

"That poor *madamin*—so young, so lovely, ending up with a sick husband."

I felt uncomfortable. It was the first time I had heard someone talk about Paolo's illness the way people always talk about such things, as a misfortune.

I discovered in that moment that Ada and I, deep down, had considered it an adventure, a destiny, a mystery, but never as something common. In this light, it was much more terrible.

"That poor thing'll lose her man, and when it's all over it'll be others who are sitting pretty in the good positions."

She spoke quickly, as erratically and as irrevocably as a clairvoyant. Then she changed her tone. "And the other two? They're also good people—boy, are they afraid!"

Now her eyes were laughing. "They'll come out without so much as a scratch in the end." Then she laughed again: "They're so afraid but they keep that girl from Monterosso around." She was laughing with her belly, tight-lipped, like a peasant woman. "One of these days she'll lead them to the house. I'd hate for that to happen, for the little ones." And she pointed at Nani, who was cautiously following the cat around the pots of evergreens.

"I hope I'm wrong, but her father—they beat him on the head. The Fascists. I know they beat him."

Paolo's affliction suddenly appeared frighteningly real to me. I wanted Sibilla to keep talking, as if it were actually given to her to know.

I studied her with my eyes: so ancient, so witchlike. What was left of that proud virago from years ago, with her cocked tricorn hat? If, then, life was so long, what would Tetto Murato be, someday, if not a far-off dream?

But when I was back on the snowy path, with Nani in my arms, I felt—just as I could feel that little girl with her warmth and her weight, feel the air on my face and the newly frozen snow crunching under my feet—all the urgency of the present.

"Do you love me, Nani?"

"Yes," she replied, without any noticeable quiver of excitement, though imbuing her answer with the kind of certainty you could count on.

XXIV

I would give my all, straining to make out what Paolo said when, in the drowsy state caused by the injections, a sudden start would jolt through him. I spoke to him for hours during the night: it was my task, and—in the dark and in the silence—communication between the two of us became natural, profound. But when he spoke "in a trance", I would feel a somewhat superstitious, morbid curiosity (which, as a matter of fact, I was ashamed of). Every time it was like I was waiting for a revelation.

As for Ada, she would come and go, with the nonchalance of a sacristan in church: she seemed disinterested, like someone who, accustomed to tending to sacred things, sees the unfolding of mysteries as routine business, and on top of that is sceptical of miracles, maybe because she considers them possible but extremely unlikely.

Every so often it was poetry that Paolo would speak in his mellow voice. Ada would pause for a second while coming or going, and would listen, before remarking disappointedly, "Virgil". Or "Baudelaire". As if to say, "Run-of-the-mill stuff."

However, from the rapt air she sometimes had while he uttered the first few lines, one might have said that she was expecting verses written by Paolo himself, perhaps in a dream.

One day—Ada and I stared at each other—it seemed as though Paolo had actually understood that someone wanted him to compose poems. Sprawled out with eyes closed, he brushed off this annoyance. "No, no. I don't write poetry."

Then, finally, he gave a sigh of relief as if he had been let off the hook, and he started speaking again, this time jokingly, as if he were talking to a friend (but it was pitiful to see him laugh that way, like someone talking to himself).

"She wanted me to write her a poem. With a dedication and everything. One to frame and show to guests." And he laughed softly, that pitiful laugh.

"Borla!" Ada shouted. She found her discovery very amusing. "It has to be her. She asked him to!"

Most of all, in these dialogues Paolo addressed a childhood friend and classmate, Aldo. Paolo had talked to me about him, about how close they had been, as something—as often happens—now faded. But Aldo was forever a great friend in his dreams.

Once, when Paolo was talking to Aldo, I heard him say my name.

It was like when the doctor, feeling your body, presses the exact spot that is diseased: in the same way I had a brief spasm, a feeling of alarm.

I was alone in the room with him. Paolo's voice was calm, grave.

"My life still rests on Ada's shoulders."

And, after a pause: "Now there's Giulia, too."

I held my breath.

"Yes, she's beautiful. But that's not it."

…

"You'll meet her."

…

"Of course she'll want to."

Now Paolo went silent. I started to say his name quietly.

"Paolo, Paolo." Then louder: "Paolo!"

He gave a start and came to while I called out to him.

"What is it?"

"You called my name."

"I did?" He smiled, but only slightly, as if to say, "Really?"

XXV

It happened that we received a visit at Tetto Murato, one that really excited Ada. Her cheerfulness could have seemed excessive, even to someone who knew her; but she had her reasons.

Maybe, most of all, what Stefano had said about her was true: that she was made for joy, for joyful cheer, for celebrations; and that her nature had been constrained—certainly not snuffed out, but a bit stifled—in a world that was too serious for her.

And so Ada was happy, for the time being, just to see somebody, and that this somebody was young, healthy, cheerful; then, because he was a partisan, a comrade who hadn't forgotten, who had travelled all that distance to see Paolo; and, lastly, because he was a doctor.

Everyone called him Lena, after some more or less Rabelaisian story, though it couldn't have been anything too bad because Lena didn't have a bad bone in his body. He was the son of rich landowners, and in his discussions with the party economists he'd often conclude, as if to cut things short, "We'll just dispossess my father." Lena had strong shoulders and a powerful chest, a big head sculpted with large proportions yet gentle, and smiling blue eyes. He had shown real talent at school, in his studies, and still did now in his profession; but he didn't seem to delve into his diagnoses, or even to take the illnesses themselves all that seriously. He almost seemed to defeat a malady by cutting it down to size.

Paolo's doctor (he had never come to Tetto Murato, with Ada often going to see him, and sometimes I went on her behalf to bring updates, or to collect prescriptions for sugar and sedatives) usually entrenched himself behind professional reticence, and he didn't appear to leave much room for hope, almost as though he considered Paolo's illness something fixed and, in a certain sense, normal, to which we could only resign ourselves. Whereas bright young Lena—even though one could suspect that he was actually more sceptical than he let on—poked fun with his beautiful big voice at that laundry list of physical ailments: "When things are this complicated, one day, out of the blue, they simply work themselves out."

Ada looked at Lena dubiously, but comforted. She was sure that if Lena stayed with them at Tetto Murato, he would be proved right about Paolo's mysterious condition.

Whereas to me it seemed that Lena was too healthy to truly understand illnesses; I thought that a doctor had to participate in some way, and not be invulnerable. But maybe the only thing Lena was really missing was the famed arrogance of doctors.

I realized that Paolo was uncomfortable, pained. Ada seemed not to notice, or she was acting as if she didn't notice. Maybe she simply wanted, for now, to take in the pleasure of Lena's visit and not be distracted; she wanted to celebrate, as was only right, his being there.

In any case, Paolo wasn't suffering because of his illness, specifically, and he wasn't looking to attract Ada's attention. No doubt, it pained him to be found inert, hidden away, by an active brother in arms. Plus, Lena was, again, too handsome, too healthy, a little like Domenica; and as with Domenica, for Paolo Lena's presence was suffocating.

To hide this oppressive feeling—so it seemed to me—and to show interest and to appear normal, Paolo asked technical questions, to which Lena tried his best to respond seriously, even though he felt like laughing.

Paolo asked, "Do you have weapons? Did they parachute in supplies?"

Lena wrapped him in his kind, clear gaze. The harshest thing he said was when he hugged him before leaving. "Bye, Professor," he said.

Ada thought it was as good an occasion as ever to get a bottle from the cellar (without forgetting to think: the owner will be reimbursed). She invited the Fantonis, too, who took advantage of the situation; they asked the doctor to take a look at Bruna's throat. In this way it came out that Lena and Bruna had known each other for a while. (Lena had been with his band in Monterosso, her hometown, which had been burned down by the Germans.) He placed his hand on her chin, then, after glancing inside her throat, affectionately ruffled her hair. He solemnly recommended—to the Fantonis' amazement—that she tie a wool sock, preferably raw wool, around her neck in the evening, "an old-time remedy".

XXVI

I delivered a letter from Stefano to Tetto Murato. In it, he thanked Paolo and Ada for keeping me company.

"That's a good one," Ada said. "Are we the ones keeping you company, or are you the one keeping us company? We should be thanking him, and instead he thanks us. Now that's really a good one."

She seemed truly perplexed, almost as though it were a question to be resolved right then and there.

Stefano also said that he would potentially be able to stay for a day or two for Christmas.

"So we'll see him," Ada concluded.

From the very beginning, Ada had never hidden her fondness for Stefano. But this fondness, and it immediately became clear to see, was different from the kind she usually felt; different from the one she harboured, for example, for the Major, about whom she often said—no one really knew why—that she "felt bad for him". When asked, she would reply, "Because he's a good person."

Now, Stefano was certainly good, but not in the same way as the Major; and yet Stefano also made her "feel bad for him".

Paolo told me once, "You know why, Giulia? Because he's your husband. Still, you realize how highly she thinks of you. It's that she's found a correspondence between the two of them: maybe between what she considers her task and his."

With me as well, when speaking about Stefano Ada often referenced her discovery—that the two of them were "the same".

Both of them, for example, had read the same book of short stories, and had both loved it; they even shared the same favourite story from the collection. (The story was *The Great Stone Face*.)

Paolo had pointed out—so as to fluster Ada—that these literary affinities didn't mean much, especially since what they were dealing with was a universally admired work; to which she then replied, with an air of mystery, "Well, actually, I know that they mean a whole lot…" By which it was clear that she was, in her indirect way, referring to something else altogether, to much more.

XXVII

I was sure that the cousins would find it unsuitable that for Christmas—and with all the trouble the whole thing entailed—Stefano and I were planning to spend a night at Tetto Murato; but I imagined they would assign all the blame to me, and to Stefano only the weakness of giving in to my whims. When Stefano was there, I never felt any regret or uncertainty; I felt vouched for by him.

Even though he didn't know the way, Stefano walked in front of me, since he was lighting the path with his torch. It was snowing, and in the disc of light I saw Stefano's feet sink into the fresh layer of snow, thick as a blanket. As I followed the little circle of light, and maybe because I was behind Stefano, I felt, in that boundless night, not lost, but rather, protected, as though I had wound up in an enclosed and safe place.

I thought to myself along the way about why I had wanted to bring Stefano to Tetto Murato. First and foremost, to offer Stefano the warmth of a real home, of a real family. This need was profound, the need to fill something waiting to be filled, while I sensed that after—if there ever was an after—it would no longer be possible, for the two of us, to be just kids. A certainty nevertheless confused, deferred in time. And it was also something that I was bringing to them, to Ada most of all.

This mysterious journey—our muffled steps on the velvet snow and the ghostly nothingness all around us—ended like in one of Andersen's tales, in Tetto Murato's warm and smoky kitchen.

Everyone came to greet us at the front door. Domenica was holding the lamp; she stood with her mouth and her eyes wide open, though there was no telling whether in amusement or alarm: as if the three kings had arrived at Tetto Murato.

Ada, silent but glowing, seemed to be thinking: "You see—I knew this would happen." And Paolo—Paolo was there too—looked excited, like he was, I thought, truly happy.

Someone grabbed the kindling, but there clearly wasn't enough for a fire. I ran down to the cellar—I liked seeing as though I knew my way around Tetto Murato in Stefano's eyes—then Paolo joined me with the lamp and, while helping me, he grazed my hand. Already trembling from the cold, I felt myself tremble even more; but Paolo was already lighting the way farther ahead, calling me.

The Fantonis also made a big fuss and immediately got ready to listen to "the bearer of news", especially the Major. Stefano told some stories, as everyone had been anticipating: stories of life in the city, and all the while he looked pale among everyone's flushed faces, paler than Paolo even. I listened like everyone else, and I liked the people in those stories. (The poor woman who after a bombing ran through the streets shouting that they had stolen her "marble stone"—her marble tabletop, symbol of bourgeois comfort, the only valuable possession in her home.)

The Fantonis sat looking at Stefano, entranced; Anna Laura stared intently with her big dark eyes, just like the "princess who never smiled".

This time, when we started to head upstairs, the Fantonis didn't ask questions. In the bedroom, we all waited for Ada to speak.

"I think we can still squeeze a bit more," she said. From the look on Stefano's face, he must have felt like he had just walked into a fairytale: he was attentive, but deferential.

Since he had confessed that he often used to fall out of bed as a child, it was decided that Stefano would take a spot in the middle of the bed.

With the light out, Ada had just enough time to say, "How lucky we are," and there was silence.

I thought Stefano had fallen asleep too, but I didn't dare check by saying his name, or by touching his hand, with him turned into a stranger in that bed at Tetto Murato.

I tried to distinguish between their breathing as they slept. Paolo's breathing was imperceptible; Ada's, big in sleep and so unlike her, and yet there was something recognizably hers about it: because it expressed assurance, and also a sensuality that was secret and at the same time trusting.

Stefano rolled over, with one of the brusque movements he made when gripped by a dream. His sleep was agitated, but deep. When Paolo's stifled groans woke Ada, who was accustomed to noticing them even in her sleep, Stefano didn't hear a thing; nor did he when Ada turned on the lamp and, swiftly and nimbly—without showing, unlike the other times, any sign of sleepiness—prepared and then gave the injection. After Paolo had entreated her, "Leave the light on for a bit—I think they're sleeping. I'll turn it off," Ada, in order not to disturb him, placed a foot on a chair and leapt over his body to get back to her place between him and Stefano. As she took flight in her sky-blue nightgown, Stefano suddenly opened his eyes. He looked astonished, like someone who had just woken up in the middle of the *One Thousand and One Nights*.

He sat up in the bed and looked around sullenly, apparently not recognizing the place; in the meantime, Ada lay down by his side. "Sorry, Stefano—Paolo's condition has no regard for guests. But now we can go right back to bed." And she was already migrating towards sleep, without noticing the way Stefano was looking at her. I realized that he didn't understand, that he didn't remember; I knew how difficult it was for him sometimes, breaking away from a dream. I took his hand in mine, but he pushed it away, and fell, grumbling, back down.

I laughed, all to myself; because Ada was asleep, and Paolo was lying exhausted with his eyes closed.

XXVIII

When we left Tetto Murato the following morning, it seemed as if we weren't actually moving away from it, as if we were roaming through a maze. We could see nothing but white: sumptuous, sparkling. Every branch, every twig, was encrusted with pearly needles, and the light itself—diffused—was as white as snow. And the impression given by the whole was enigmatic, impenetrable.

We left the old road where the snow was deep and untouched, and took the byroad, which was longer but easier to walk on, already marked out with tracks; it reconnected to the main road which the Germans usually cleared of snow. (They travelled along it in their tanks and their light eastern infantry carts.) It was no longer a maze as it had been along the paths, but a dazzling desert, under the rising sun.

I was squeezing Stefano's big, dry hand, and listening to him tell me about the dream that had agitated him the night before.

"All of us, even if we hadn't collaborated, had to go down to hell. We were guilty of not having acted, of not having done enough to help our brothers and sisters. They made us walk down these flights of stairs (the stairs to the bomb shelters, I'm guessing), which were dark and steep. Down at the bottom, hell was a kind of brothel. Real ones have always disgusted me, and the scary thing here was that all the women were people I knew. There was Nuccia, poor thing, in her very high heels; Lydia, who still hadn't given her arrogance a rest and was walking around like she owned the place; Nene, who seemed to be playing the victim as per usual. I was already feeling distressed, when it dawned on me that you might be there too. I started looking around in a frenzy—sure, they were familiar faces, but I wasn't interested in them. That's when I nearly have a heart attack: I see Signora Ada." (Stefano always referred to her in that way, out of respect, he said.) "Once she sees me, she starts celebrating my being there, the way she does, laughing, and I feel like slapping some sense into her. Suddenly, I realize I'm in bed and I see her in a see-through nightgown nearly jumping on top of me and then starting to lie down at my side. In that moment I felt tempted; my head was spinning a bit. But I didn't dare move. I saw that room, it looked like I was in their house. I saw the oil lamp, a mirror. Then a hand touched me; I pushed it away, and that was enough. Everything changed."

XXIX

Stefano had to leave again. This entailed, I knew, spending two nights in the cold and the stench of the train station's waiting area, if not in the shelter—first in our hometown and then in Turin. What came next, I couldn't imagine: Stefano didn't share all of the unpleasantness with me.

At Tetto Murato, I found Paolo weighed down. Ada seemed quiet, uneasy.

Back at the beginning of December, they had killed, in a horrifying manner, one of the partisan leaders, a friend. Paolo was kept in the dark about it—Ada hadn't wanted to tell him—but every so often he would ask about this friend, of all people: it seemed as though he had sensed the truth, and Ada would look at him in those moments with fear in her eyes. A superstitious fear, it seemed to me.

At night Paolo didn't sleep, but he didn't feel like talking with me either, as he usually did.

I had almost always needed to fight off sleep during those long nights in which we spoke softly to each other; or rather, I didn't really put up a fight, but would suddenly succumb to an onslaught of sleep, kept at bay for too long and grown wrathful.

I'd stammer, losing my ability to pronounce words, and to think them. Often, I would either plunge into a deep slumber, or my own annoyance at having given in to sleep would wake me. When that happened, I'd start talking again; then Paolo would say, kindly but firmly, "Go to sleep now, Giulia."

Sometimes I woke in the middle of the night; if everything was calm, if, after listening a little while, I deduced that Paolo was sleeping also or at least wasn't showing any sign of being awake and hoping to talk, I would quietly slip out of the room. I would wrap myself in something woolly or even my fur coat, but on the landing the cold sank its claws into me. I'd go halfway down the stairs, and I'd stand for a while in front of a little window—with no pane—facing the countryside. I saw, below, a little square garden, buried under the snow: the short branches of the hedge, the scattered black spots of bushes and shrubs tracing linear patterns. It was just like a little cemetery, and it gave, of death, an image that was poor, calm and solemn. I'd look at it for as long as I could bear the cold; and I felt I was grasping a little bit of the ultimate sense of things.

XXX

One night—Ada was sleeping restlessly, which was unusual for her, sighing and twitching in the bed—Paolo and I listened to distant shots in the night.

Paolo recalled that it was the last night of the year—we wouldn't have remembered otherwise—and how it was a German custom to celebrate in that way. But even as I thought that there was no battle, no killings, that unruly swarm of gunfire was no less harrowing. It actually had something convulsive to it, desperate; it sounded anxious and, at the same time, determined—though it seemed to come from men not on the eve of some ordeal, but desertion and degradation.

Paolo stayed quiet; he was feeling, I could sense it, the same thing I was. Even if he had spoken, he likely wouldn't have gone beyond objectively considering the nature of that custom. I was sure that he, too, had to struggle with a temptation to give in, to let go of everything. It was just about unbearable, the sensation of being able to understand—almost as an unknown, unhuman language—the meaning of that tumult.

I didn't want him to speak; maybe I was afraid that Paolo might be different then: closer, but less strong.

And, in the end, I felt it as a kind of comfort, his strength not to say anything in that moment, and it became my strength, too.

The shots became less frequent and, after one last brief and clamorous rush, stopped.

Tears, which I hadn't felt coming, started running down my face: gently, like thawing snow. It could have been an admission of weakness, and thereby the very thing someone, at one time or another, would have tried to console: because that is the way weeping often is. But the best is the solitary kind, which is sufficient unto itself, and is almost a form of strength; it acts, in fact, as strength because it cleanses, washing away waste, the dribble of weakness.

XXXI

It was right around then that the news came about Irma. It was announced by the children, by the maids, it echoed throughout Tetto Murato. But when I arrived, no one spoke of it in the kitchen, no one thought to tell me. It was Nani who planted herself in front of me and, looking me straight in the eyes, almost scrutinizing me, asked me gravely, "Did you know that Irma died?"

Nani had spoken solemnly because that was the way she was, but I felt embarrassed, as if the serious look in her eyes were actually inquisitorial, and not knowing Irma had died amounted to being guilty.

It was no doubt a product of Nani's own particular zeal, her conviction that it was up to her to inform "Signora Giulia" of something serious that had happened among the children.

She told me that Irma had died "because she drank lamp oil". I had no reason to doubt the accuracy of what she said. And it was by all means possible. Irma was one of the local children; I couldn't have said which one.

"What did Irma look like?"

"She had long hair," Pietruccio answered first.

"But why did she drink oil?"

"They gave it to her as medicine," Domenica explained. "Because oil cleans. She couldn't digest it, and the oil burned her up inside. She screamed and screamed."

Domenica wasn't Nani, and so the story was blown to new proportions; and yet her voice conveyed restraint, a kind of modesty that was out of character. Her blue eyes were full of tears, and she was biting her lips, fighting back sobs. The children were all around her, gripping onto the end of her clothes, and they looked like they were all her children.

"Did you go to pray for Irma?" she shouted. Then, frightened, the children ran all together to pray where they had laid Irma.

"Just think," Ada said, "what they did. They killed her."

"Just think," she kept repeating, stressing each word; "they made her drink oil." Then, unexpectedly: "It's my fault. I should have been checking to see what they gave her." She paused to listen. "They're mourning her. Do you hear it?"

I heard, over the rumbling of the stove, over Paolo's laboured breathing, their wailing; it was like hearing a chorus of frogs at night, harmoniously dissonant, rough yet clear: similar to that sound, but human. Much more human, I thought, than the sinister swarm of gunfire a few nights before. "They're able to grieve like that," I thought, "for the very fact that they don't know oil burns."

But I didn't say so. I knew that Ada would only have scowled and railed against them: "Then they should stop—stop grieving and learn that oil burns."

When Paolo's breathing had become more relaxed, he also asked me, "Did you hear about the little girl?" He already had a hunch, because he then said, "You know that Ada thinks it's her fault?" And added, "In fact, it is our fault."

I had the sensation that he had guessed my thoughts and then responded, as he often did, without following me, but making me follow him instead.

That night with Irma, none of us could find any peace. But the person we might have feared would be the most upset, Nani, was actually the only one who was calm.

"Since Irma died," she said, "that means I won't die tonight. Right, Mamma?"

"Of course," Ada replied, "you won't die." She didn't say it jokingly like the other nights, nor tenderly, at least not on the outside; she had spoken almost violently.

Paolo didn't express any annoyance over the sound of the wailing, but his suffering was visibly heightened by it.

For him, that dirge was no easier to bear than the gunfire: that was a game, after all, absurd and sad like violence in children; but the lament was feminine and sensual, "all too human".

It seemed, little by little, that we were taking part in that lament: that we were like children kept awake by their own crying.

XXXII

Now I would play a game along the way to Tetto Murato. I tried to make stretches of the road—from one bridge to the next, from a house to a tree—coincide with a given number of Hail Marys or Our Fathers. I pretended it was a game, and in the meantime I was praying.

I had started, at first, without being aware of it; then, as I realized what I was murmuring, an emotion ran through me: not exactly surprise, but what someone might feel when—perhaps in a dream—she finds herself in a familiar but forgotten place, a place where she had once been happy (or not), and meanwhile wonders, though not right away, how she ended up back there. The first time that a prayer rose almost of its own accord to my lips wasn't on the road there, but at Tetto Murato. When the snow hadn't come yet, in the afternoon Ada would go to the school on her bicycle, while I stayed on my own at Paolo's bedside. The Major was also there, that time, on the other side of the bed, for the injection. Paolo was having an asthma attack that seemed like it would never end. Suspended, almost hanging from the ceiling by an invisible thread, he was standing up on the mattress, straining his whole body in an effort to push himself higher and higher in search of air, his head tilted slightly to the side, just like a hanged man.

Our eyes—mine and the Major's—met. It was then that I said softly, hurriedly, a prayer. Had it been his round, kind eyes that suggested it to me? The Fantonis were very devout people. On the stairs, Ada had pointed out the row of holy images on the windowsill—turned towards the window—put there to ward off outside dangers (they counterbalanced, I noticed, the painting hanging above our door: a portrait of Mazzini).

That prayer, and the ones I usually said by now during my walks, were humble, dictated by my fears.

I prayed for Paolo, but not "on his behalf"; I knew that nothing in him wavered. I asked for help against physical pain, against his illness.

I wondered about Ada, if she too was, in some vulnerable part of her being, actually afraid. Needless to say, she didn't pray.

Before meeting Paolo, she had been a practising believer; then she had transferred her whole self to his world. She started to think like him, or at least the way she imagined he did—Paolo had never said a word to her about religion.

Was it safe to say that Ada had lost her faith? More likely, she didn't even need to pray, her faith was so great.

XXXIII

And so I said prayers—not continuously, but by phony chance as I followed the game. In the meantime, I didn't take my eyes off the road, which by now had been reduced to a roughly beaten trail, or off the few scattered farmhouses sunk into the snow, grey with a sickly pallor, spotted with dark splotches of smoke and manure. In the other seasons they were hidden by the trees. Sometimes a house which had a pine tree would stick out; and it would seem less desolate, almost rich and lush.

I also played more straightforward games. I would break with my foot the thin layer of snow over the grooves left by the carts. The slight pop and the squeaky crackle filled me with a joy that was an echo of games long-gone and forgotten. On the deep ditches along the sides of the road, the crust of ice was very thick, and withstood the repeated kicking of my heel; at most the surface would crack, though below other layers resisted, thin but dense. Or else its entire weight would cave in with a groan, a kind of hissing sound, which gave no joy. After, I'd observe from up close the geometric intricacies, which were meticulous, wondrous; and I felt confusion at the thought that I had crudely violated—like an invading soldier in a church—a detail in the immense building that winter had erected all around.

One time I broke off an icicle shaped like a sword with an elegant hilt. The cold burned my hand even through my glove, but I wanted to bring it to Nani. Nani opened her eyes wide at the sight of it, but she didn't appreciate it as much as the squirrel I had bought at the market, once she learned that there was no way to preserve it.

On sunny days, the desert of snow was beautiful, as were the hemispherical dunes, a metamorphosis of the mounds of rocks along the roadside. Here and there brambles emerged, black and unkempt like miniature forests.

I held my breath for a second when arriving at Tetto Murato. The silence enveloped—more compact than the snow—the semi-buried houses, and the great black pine tree, in its infinite melancholy, seemed simultaneously to point to and to hide a secret. Before going upstairs, I would peek through the little window and eavesdrop on what was happening in the kitchen. I did this to put myself at ease, and yet I knew that whatever might happen, or be about to happen upstairs, there wouldn't be any commotion foreshadowing it in the kitchen. If I saw only the children and the maids, I'd stop for a moment in the doorway. Sometimes I entered, sneaking Nani a kiss.

When they didn't notice me, I liked spying on the kitchen even more. I would walk in, close the door behind me, and for a while no one, except for maybe Bruna, or Anna Laura, who were the most attentive, would notice me there.

Once, Nani and Pietruccio were sitting close to each other, squeezed onto the same chair, dangling their little shoeless feet in rough wool socks, apparently waiting for something.

Domenica was fiddling near the woodstove; then, cursing, she pulled something out of the oven: the two children's shoes. She had put them in to dry because the two of them were always complaining that their feet were cold and wet. They weren't of good quality, were wartime shoes, and now they came out of the oven worn and partly scorched. The children gaped at them, puzzled, and also a little frightened by Domenica's shouting: "Now you'll go tell your whores of mothers what's happened!" And meanwhile, with her back to me, she was giving vigorous whacks and shoving the poor shoes back onto their feet.

XXXIV

I had come to the conclusion that Ada not only wasn't truly afraid, but that she was more tormented by their money problems than by the obscure course of Paolo's illness. Like anyone who isn't a dreamer, she gave precedence to the issue that needed an immediate solution, and that depended on her.

I tried to suggest that they let his old companions know the situation Paolo was in, but Ada—she had probably thought of it too and mentioned it to him—replied that Paolo had told her that the party wasn't a charity.

Giving my own character a shove, I decided to act. I wrote to that woman Borla from the lunch out in the hills.

One morning some time thereafter (I had spent the night at Tetto Murato and was helping Ada make the bed), I realized that Ada wanted to tell me something. Paolo had left us alone for a minute (even if he had been feeling unwell up till a moment before, he would still always walk down the stairs by himself to the first landing, where there was a door unlike the others, with a single rather than a double panel, which jutted out slightly from the wall—he never wanted to hear any nonsense about contraptions and tools from the good old days, which were in no short supply at Tetto Murato).

So, Ada was making the bed, and she was tugging at the sheets made of fine but frayed linen. She was doing it with particular care, because Paolo hated it when they loosened. I was helping her, following her movements, when I realized—I looked directly at her face since she had gone quiet—that she seemed on her guard about something. She said, under her breath, though with a cold, detached tone that was strange for her, "Borla sent money."

I gave a slight jump, and immediately felt guilty: clearly Ada was not in the least bit pleased. Awkwardly, I asked, "What did Paolo say?" "I didn't tell him." I stayed silent. "She sent it via the parish priest, and she wrote a grumpy letter." "How come?" "You know how jealous she is. She says that we forgot about her, that she'd been left completely in the dark, and so on. Seems like someone talked to her about us."

I gathered all of my courage. "It was me."

"It was you," Ada repeated seriously, sounding so unlike herself that it left me utterly at a loss. At the same time, I understood that in forgetting about Borla's famed jealousy, I had got under her skin by writing to her.

I measured—the way we measure a wide gap opening up at our feet more with our own dizziness, our nausea, than with our eyes—what Ada had called the "differentness" of Signora Borla and of her world, and this finally allowed me to taste the privileged isolation of Tetto Murato, more than the desert of snow ever had, more than the silence around the houses.

Even a helping hand, a fraternal gesture, could not be simple if it came from that other world, and instead threw things into turmoil. The letter was hidden away, like an undetonated explosive.

XXXV

Nowadays Paolo would often groan and thrash about, invoking the little girl as though she were in danger, and calling out to Ada for help: "Ada! Be careful! Do you know what the girl's doing? Don't leave her alone!" Sometimes he would shout, though with a husky, choked voice, "Oh God! The pin!" (In his nightmare, he was witnessing the event unfold all over again.)

When opening his eyes with a start and seeing that Nani was next to the bed—Ada had got her to come upstairs in the meantime—he would say hello to her, and he would be happy, surprised to find her there, but he wouldn't seem to feel in seeing her completely safe and sound the kind of relief that might have been expected after thinking she was in danger only a second earlier.

Ada, like me, thought that all his concern for Nani was concealing—unconsciously—another concern of his.

Ada would freeze before this thought as before a secret of which she was the keeper, although it did not belong to her—a secret into which she did not even have the right to enquire.

I didn't say a thing. I couldn't tell her that while talking at night Paolo revealed that it was precisely for her that he was so distressed: for her health.

For that matter, Paolo often pleaded with her, "Ada, cover yourself up some more, you'll catch a cold." "But I'm perfectly comfortable," was her reply, and she let out one of her musical sighs, almost weighed down by too much tenderness. Then she turned to me. "Believe it or not, Giulia, but I don't really feel much of a difference with these things; I'm rather rugged, actually."

At night, Paolo always began by talking about Ada.

"You know, Giulia," he said, "Ada's not that strong. She's not as strong as she seems."

And, "You see how much she needs her sleep; who can say if she's also starving most of the time, because that's something she's able to hide."

And, "Regardless, we would have been far from well off, almost poor actually, but at least I could have worked."

Or, "I couldn't... couldn't not try to do something. Now I wonder if I even had the right, since I wasn't alone."

He ended by saying, "If we make it out of this, we'll pick things back up with our old life, and she'll be happy all the same; but sometimes I think that we'll never get there. I'm afraid she'll get sick."

I felt a sense of bewilderment hearing Paolo say these things, and the very sweetness of his confiding in me was painful. Because Paolo's fears concerning Ada's health seemed like a sign to me, proof of the dimming, the near disappearance in him, of his meagre will to live. As though Paolo talked about Ada not only out of compassion for her, but out of modesty, so as not to talk about himself. And an equally or even more serious sign seemed to be the awareness, which I believed—feared—I could glimpse in him, of a futility buried at the heart of the struggle he had taken part in.

I received a letter from Stefano, in which he talked at length about friends—usually he didn't go beyond asking for news and sending regards—eventually arriving at the point. It was something he felt he had to share with me immediately, instead of waiting for the next time we met. (Now that Stefano was farther away, his letters were delivered to me by hand by a company courier, and thereby escaped censorship.)

He said that he had been warned by a dream, and what followed was his account of the dream.

"I had to take Signora Ada to a funeral. She wasn't ready and was taking forever to get dressed. She'd go off into another room and come back wearing something new each time, a hat, or gloves, and show it off to me. She wanted me to see how good she looked and to compliment her, with that not-altogether-innocent coquetry of hers. She was practically wearing a riding outfit, with an ostrich feather on her hat, which quivered as she turned abruptly about. I was on edge because we were going to be late, and I also would have liked for her to behave more appropriately. In the meantime, I'm becoming more and more convinced that the funeral we need to go to is her husband's. I realize that she's unaware of this. We're running really late, and we have to get to the funeral at the cemetery. She keeps getting distracted on the way there, looking into shop windows, talking about clothes. The cemetery is very far away, and we've wasted so much time it's already evening when we do get there. She starts kicking up a fuss about something, very seriously, the way she does in real life, without realizing how charming she is in those moments. She's complaining about cemeteries, maybe criticizing the fact that people bury the dead.

"I kept thinking that she didn't know why we were there. A group of people was blocking the work of the gravediggers. It was getting dark. No one noticed us there. But she recognized some friends of Paolo's. I feared, and almost hoped, too (so that it wouldn't be up to me to tell her), that she'd realize what was taking place; but she only realized that it was a funeral for a Resistance fighter, and she started shouting that someone needed to give a eulogy, that Paolo would give it. 'Why isn't Paolo there?' And then she's shouting, 'Paolo! Paolo!'

"I was looking at her with pity, rather frightened. By now she had changed a lot; her hair was messy, she was poorly dressed, her eyes had a terrible light in them. You would have said that, deep down, she knew, and she didn't want to admit the truth. I felt so distraught that I woke up shivering (in my already freezing-cold bed)."

The dream, along with his fears—the dream having been inspired, brought to life by nothing other than those fears—over Paolo's obscure illness, had left Stefano with the suspicion that Ada was just as oblivious as she had been in the dream. In order to act in some way, to offer, for the time being, the only available solution to what could potentially happen—and could not be ruled out from happening—though also to ease somewhat his own anxiety, he concluded: "If, God forbid, it really does happen, and she ends up on her own, then we'll take her in with us, her and the girl."

There was the comforting assurance of recognizing Stefano in this. And it was a consolation to be able to think of at least a minimal provision that we could take against the threat of something so terrible. But it was also—if Stefano had thought all this—confirmation of the threat itself.

I didn't believe that Paolo could actually die; and yet I could "see" vividly what would have happened "after".

I regretted that I hadn't recognized—predicted—Stefano's worried thinking: now I couldn't say a word about it.

And so it was a secret, one founded on thoughts that were kind, but not hopeful.

XXXVI

From then on, I noticed signs of tiredness in Ada. Physical tiredness, exhaustion, which caused her to heave a sigh every now and then, nothing more.

And the fact that she was, in some way, oblivious, as in Stefano's dream, made her pitiable, almost tragic in my eyes, which were always following her.

Until one night (Paolo had been silently holding out in the grip of his pain; but if a groan slipped out from his lips, then Ada was already up, practically apologizing like a watchman who had dozed off), a night when I had wanted to call her myself for some time, even though I knew how much she desperately needed sleep, and when she was slow to wake because she was too tired—on that night, she reached the peak of her selflessness. She lit the oil lamp, seemingly as she always did, her hands making vague but not indecisive movements: imprecise, as though from inexperience, but resolute (like the hands of someone who lovingly wraps a bandage around a wound but doesn't know how it's done, and wraps it tight, even too tight, though it will soon slacken). And all of her, in her flowing, fanciful nightgown, as she held the lamp in front of her face, her eyes opened wide, looked like a painting that shone for an instant: almost as though she were not the one holding the lamp, but Ada as goddess, as sacred dancer, revealed by a light reflected off the wall of a dark temple.

A thud on the floor, a sharp burst: the lamp. Ada said meekly, "I was asleep."

I felt keen regret over the loss of that beautiful lamp, and also keen pity for Ada, who had got up in her sleep, and whose fingers hadn't had a good grip; pity that was identical to regret, as if Ada herself had in some way shattered.

XXXVII

More snow fell, and more snow still. The silence enwrapping the room bound it ever more tightly; the dull, weak light of the short days no longer stretched all the way to reach Paolo's bed; only the folded-down end of the sheet reflected the white outside and spread an equal sadness.

We couldn't fight the dusk with the lamplight, due to the usual need to save oil. The woodstove could no longer be kept lit for the whole day either, because the supply of sawdust was running low and there seemed to be no chance of refilling it.

Since Paolo hadn't noticed and wasn't bothered by it, Ada pretended to forget to ask Domenica to light the stove which, once lit, went until it burned up everything.

When she was alone with Domenica, who was naturally aware of the issue and, in fact, was the one who went to the sawmill, Ada would try to ask her opinion.

"What should I do, Domenica?"

Domenica would stand still with her columnlike legs spread slightly apart, staring into space for a moment with her brow furrowed as if in thought, and would inevitably reply:

"I really don't know what to tell you."

There wasn't a hint of complacency in her words, nor in the way she said them; yet that sentence, which both reasserted Domenica's freedom to wash her hands of the problem and alluded to the irreparability of the problem itself, came across as cruel to Ada, as well as annoying (to the extent that even she was capable of getting annoyed); though certainly Domenica hadn't meant to poke fun at the situation, nor would she have known how. Her person exuded physical solidity and equilibrium, but it was wrong to expect some kind of life lesson, too; just as one shouldn't ask for oracles from the simple natural world. At most, Domenica, with the good intention of wanting to contribute, would sometimes let out a quick sigh of regret.

Ada soon gave up on trying to scheme with Domenica, even though it would have been a small comfort. She went back simply to hoping that something would happen.

As it had stopped snowing, a freezing cold fell on the countryside and on the houses.

Ada had no choice but to keep the woodstove continuously lit; and as she watched the sawdust being shovelled in— Domenica did it, giving resolute heaves—it was as if she were watching bread flour being thrown into the fire.

I asked to see the remaining heap, tucked away in the front hall. It looked to me like there was still a lot left; but Domenica, who knew better, declared without even having to think about it that there was enough for a week at most.

XXXVIII

Paolo was more uneasy than ever before. So uneasy that Ada started to anticipate, to fear, she couldn't say what, but she feared it, and she kept a close eye on him.

This constant surveillance, which consisted of rapid glances that wanted to appear distracted, did not go unnoticed, and drove Paolo to his limit; the idea that Ada would play a part in torturing him, that she would reinforce the walls of his prison, was too much for him to take.

The pain had dwindled for the time being; but no less excruciating was his restlessness, a feeling of suffocation and, ultimately, a desperate urge to flee.

This restlessness must have given him an illusion of energy: Ada walked into the room to find him feverishly dressing himself.

She was alarmed, nearly frightened, but didn't say anything. Since Paolo wasn't looking at her but did seem in a hurry, she risked asking, with the particular imprudence she showed in certain moments, "Do you want me to help you?"

"No need, thank you."

Paolo had responded with affected politeness, like a stranger; with a quick, cold smile.

Ada pushed her luck further. She spoke kindly, making another mistake:

"Do you feel like going downstairs?"

"And why shouldn't I feel like it?"

And with a voice that was no longer sharp, but cracked, almost hoarse from emotion: "Of course—you should, actually!"

But when he had her hand him his coat, and started to button it with his bloodless, frenzied fingers, she couldn't stop herself from shouting, "Are you going outside?"

"I need air," he replied. "I can't take it in here any longer."

Ada moved aside as he came headlong towards the door, rushing uncertainly like a wounded man, and she listened to him go down the stairs, hoping that he would run into their daughter—who knows? Anything that might stop him—because certainly he wouldn't be turning back. When she couldn't hear him any more, she went down to the kitchen to follow his movements from the little window onto the road. I was in the kitchen playing with Nani. I understood from Ada's face that something was happening that was even worse than running out of sawdust.

Ada took me by the hand, and since we couldn't see anything from the window, so high was the snow, we went outside. Paolo was walking off in the direction of the river, struggling with each step to lift his foot once it had sunk into the snow. Now and then he would stop, panting for air.

Ada started to follow him, just as she was, without even covering herself up; I didn't dare move.

We felt, deep down, a vague fear that Paolo had gone a bit mad, but foremost in both of us was our worry that he could get sick from the cold.

It was a dark day outside, and only off the snow did light ricochet up towards the low, dull sky.

The way he looked—his buttoned-up coat, his thick head of hair, his beard (he had a beard now), and all of the snow around him—reminded me of something. I recognized an image that had enchanted me as a child, a photograph of a painting: *Tolstoy en route vers l'infini*. The only thing missing was the classic Russian sack flung over his shoulder.

Suddenly I felt anger in me, directed at Paolo; and, at the same time, I felt sorry for him, so unlike himself in that moment—and yet the symbol of himself—and ultimately for all of us, as if we had truly wound up with no home, no warmth, truly lost out there in all that snow.

Ada was trying to persuade him. "Wait for a warmer day, then you can go out. Come back inside, please."

Paolo didn't answer. And we could see that he didn't feel free there either, but still trapped, powerless.

Ada, her head down, trudged back with long and slow strides.

Driven by a somewhat childish, convulsive desperation, I ran out, hopping, leaping, until I reached Paolo. I was practically on top of him, and I sobbed into his face, "Paolo, stop torturing us, come inside."

In the room, back in bed, he said to me—and his voice was calm once again, "One should never resort to violence."

But I didn't want to understand. "What violence?"

XXXIX

The next day Paolo was in an extreme state of weakness and prostration, not desperately on edge but rather, mild-mannered, meek even. The restlessness of the day before had left him completely. It was as though he had been bled dry: he was cold to the touch.

Ada watched what was left of the sawdust disappear into the woodstove, and I could see from her face that her heart was breaking. But as soon as the stove started to spread its last warmth, already she had moved beyond feeling discouraged, already she was saying, "Good, for today we're all set."

Even though the stove had been lit earlier than usual—for a final show of splendour—Paolo couldn't shake off the cold; nor did the little food he'd managed to get down seem to provide him with any warmth.

We had lain down fully dressed (as we often did in the almost perennially cold bedroom) under the fur blanket. We were just about ready to sleep, dead tired as we were.

In an exhausted, kind voice, Paolo said, "Ada, come close to me, please. Warm me up a bit."

Ada hopped out of the bed with the urgency with which she

always flew into action, slipped off her clothes and lay down next to Paolo. "Thank you," Paolo said.

"Your hand is like ice!" Ada shouted. At that point I also moved closer, took his other hand in mine.

"Are you warming up a little?" Ada asked.

"Thanks, yes, a little."

We stayed like that for a while without speaking, Paolo's icy hands in our warm hands.

Ada's hands were bigger, rougher—spoiled by work—whereas mine were "hands that had never worked a day", as Paolo had said once.

Paolo was still lying there motionless, but his cheeks had regained colour. Ada and I, sitting up slightly, looked each other in the eyes.

He smiled, in that wry way of his, both cheerful and sad.

"You can see," he said, "that I'm not an atheist."

This shook me awake. "Why?"

"An atheist is someone who doesn't need anything outside of himself, who doesn't need anyone. And I, as you two can see, can't be alone."

Ada, who was happy because Paolo seemed revived, because he was talking, pointed out, light and gay, that Paolo "didn't give much away". I thought, on the contrary, that he had revealed a great deal—the most one possibly could. But I didn't say a thing, in part because Paolo had very likely been joking: to a certain extent, he had definitely meant it as a joke.

XL

That oppressive state he was in still hadn't come to an end, when Paolo was seized by a fit of asthma. His eyes now resembled those of a sick child who looks at adults with a precocious awareness that any call for help will be useless. It was impossible to shake off the impression that his malady now wanted to "finish him off", to almost "put him out of his misery", as people say.

Ada, always theatrical in her joy, in her surprise, in her indignation, was composed then, right as she touched the limit of all hope: with the end of the war neither close nor far—outside of time—Paolo attached to life by a thread, and meanwhile, almost as a sign, the unobtainable sawdust, the unlit stove.

She moved about looking deft, serious, but not anxious, and not "mean" either, because there was not even the shadow of a game left.

At his first rasping gasps—faint, almost as though the disease itself were showing restraint—she stood still for a second, stared into Paolo's nearly stunned, questioning eyes, nearly sheepish in fact (as if he were saying: "Forgive me for this, too"), and then threw her long arms down at her sides, hunching her shoulders slightly, in the despondent gesture simple people make when surrendering to disappointment; and for a second in my eyes she was, as she bent over in that way, old.

While Ada was coming and going, Paolo called her with his eyes and with waves of his hand, his arm lying slack on the folded end of the bedsheet; once again with languid hand gestures, he mimed writing. Ada placed in front of him a little piece of paper ripped from the edge of a book cover (another day Paolo would have noticed, disapproved of such untidiness) and a pencil. It was nothing out of the ordinary; Paolo often resorted to this means of communicating with Ada during his attacks. But she didn't wait, after propping the piece of paper against the book, for Paolo to start writing, and she went downstairs for something. I stood there next to the bed, on the point of leaving (I had told the cousins I would come back that evening). I hesitated; I wasn't sure how to say goodbye to Paolo, who in the meantime had shut his eyes: unusual during his fits of asthma, because throughout he always seemed to be searching for his breath with his eyes, too.

His eyelids drooped shut, his head slumped on the pillow, he started to write slowly, not so much with difficulty as with diligence, determination.

Still sprawled there with eyes closed, he folded the paper, put it in my palm and closed my fingers around the note, like someone slipping secret charity or placing a candy in a child's hand.

Just as a child would have done, I immediately—though jealously—opened my hand, and tried to read in the room's dark twilight.

Paolo's writing was generally minute and clear; even in this message, achingly scrawled with his eyes closed, his hand was recognizable; but the letters seemed disembodied, abstract: defined but indecipherable. They were four words spaced apart. The first was maybe just a single letter like a slash, followed by a longer word; the last was the longest, and ended in marks that were so slight as to hardly be there at all.

But the first word to pop out at me was the third, *you*. The sentence became clear to me in a flash when I started to read it again from the beginning. The emotion I felt was so violent that after throwing a glance at Paolo, still blind and mute, I moved away, went down the stairs, and was out the door and on my way (Ada and I had already said goodbye for the night).

When I found myself on the snowy path, and opened my hand which was still clutching the note, I was tempted to turn back. I laughed, all alone, at myself: the note was obviously for Ada.

The last, long word was *infinitely*: a word that was curiously rhetorical and yet, in that moment, true, charged with all of the truth and desolation of the present. The second word was one that I had always believed to be the simplest and the most human word, and which now, instead, seemed vexing, ambiguous and, at the same time, violent.

It was the word that Stefano of all people didn't use, had never used, not even in our early time together and in our earliest confessions (because, he said, it had been misused too many times in the world).

Well, I knew that between Ada and Paolo—Ada had told me herself, back when Paolo was away—there had once flowed the language of lovers.

No matter what, it was late to turn back; I would return, as had been understood, the next day.

Now I walked feeling tired, a bit dazed, but calm—when a new thought suddenly sprang up before me, as plain as reality. Paolo must have felt that it was my hand, my fingers which he had lightly but resolutely closed around his secret note.

But even this new certainty was short-lived, and I wouldn't have been able to say whether, in feeling it crumble, I experienced disappointment or relief.

I decided to destroy the note—faced with the possibility that Ada might not recognize it as intended for her.

I tore the thin paper into small pieces and let them fall, fluttering slowly, onto the snow.

Only, I thought that it was sad to get rid of a sign of him, which I could have also held on to as it was, ambiguous. I felt regret and anger towards myself. I also felt exhausted, my legs sore and heavy. I was afraid I had fallen ill, that I wouldn't be able to go back the next day.

XLI

Instead, the next day was a joyful one.

Everything had already happened when I arrived at Tetto Murato.

Entering the room, I saw everything just as I'd left it, with Paolo still in bed, but then Ada ran up to me like in better days, victorious: "Look!"

I looked and still didn't understand. She pointed to the woodstove: it was lit. That morning Domenica had called her and had asked her calmly, as if it weren't a big deal, "You want sawdust or not?"

Ada flew outside as she was—that is, in her robe—into the snow. Outside, the middle-aged peasant, who was thin and of small stature, and his cart with the sawdust were waiting motionless: black and solitary in the immense white.

The man looked at her, Ada said, petrified; he blinked, and a certain amount of trepidation was still on his face after they spoke.

Ada said that she would never forget that man; he was stamped so clearly in her memory that, she said, she surely "could draw him".

★

During the nights the air was freezing, hard like glass, but the stream in front of the houses had started to flow again.

Paolo went downstairs to the kitchen for meals; and now, just when the dinners had gone back to being cheerful, I would more rarely stay for the evening.

That return, I feared, would push me away, would in a sense take me back to the past. The days were getting longer, and Paolo was doing better: and so there was no good reason for me to stay.

Paolo, as if sensing this, said every evening while taking my hand, "Come back tomorrow."

I was grateful to him for this, as if it were true that I otherwise wouldn't have dared come back the next day.

I could imagine how Ada would have made fun of me if she knew: "You still need to be told?" or "With everything I need to worry about, I also have to remember to invite you!"

I stayed for dinner and then for the night at Tetto Murato only if Ada told me the day before, "Make sure you stay over tomorrow"—even though I knew that the following day Ada wouldn't remember having said it, and, furthermore, that she said it or not for no real reason, other than that maybe she did or didn't hope that the next day they would have butter or lard or wheat bread.

Then when Ada placed in front of me a slice of bread, the biggest of all, I'd nibble and swallow it with veneration, not only because it was good, but because I knew it was one thing less for the community at Tetto Murato.

The truth was that everything, like the season, was slowly changing. And I was scared, frightened, because I feared—deep down, I knew—that I wasn't ready, wasn't prepared to change: to accept that something was changing.

Paolo's presence, while signalling a return to normal, also spread an air of severity, almost an awkwardness, as if we were hosting an honourable but unfamiliar guest, a foreigner.

The Major still didn't take the liberty of asking his opinion about the latest news from London Radio, while his wife talked under her breath with Ada, and the maids, like the children, tried not to make any noise.

Paolo kept his eyes on Nani, interested only in her; he would smile at the others so they too could witness how amusingly serious Nani was when she ate.

Nani ate with the same aristocratic manners as Ada, but not with her speedy detachment (nor did she forcibly apply herself as Ada had done at that lunch with Borla, which was also a kind of detachment). Nani was fully present in her task, and we could see that she considered it not only an important but a welcome one too. She chewed slowly, almost ritually, as if to draw from the food all of its goodness—you could have said, all of its possible significance.

In this context, Nani certainly didn't appear fragile, nor did she seem her usual cautious or quizzical self. She kept a hand curved around her plate and seemed solid, avid, devoted, and all the while dignified.

Paolo would try to get a reaction out of her, never succeeding in throwing off her calm and intense diligence; she'd simply turn to look at him, without laughing or losing her patience.

Once, after the soup had just been served, Nani ran with the other children to the door—there was a knocking sound, but it had been a prank pulled by Bruna—and when she came back to her place at the table, she found her plate was missing (hidden by Paolo).

Nani's surprise was great, as was her concern; she looked for it meticulously, with confidence, though also with noticeable anxiety.

When Paolo put the plate back, she only said, in her usual calm fashion, though with a hint of disapproval, "I don't like pranks when it comes to food."

XLII

One evening the air outside was so fine, crystalline, it seeped with subtle puffs into the kitchen, causing the acetylene flame to flicker; the flame itself, strange and diabolic, came out hissing and forced the Major to fiddle with it patiently.

Paolo was sitting rather rigidly, absorbed in thought; I realized that Ada was keeping her eyes on him, this time without hiding it, since he didn't even see her. He was staring straight in front of him.

Following Ada's gaze, I noticed her focus move from Paolo's face to his hands. Ada gave a start when the hand Paolo was resting on the table next to his plate—he had stopped eating in the meantime—started to move, raising and lowering its middle finger, rhythmically, as if actually keeping time.

It was a sign. Sure enough, it was not long before Paolo stood up and, in the silence that formed around his abrupt movement, walked to the door with the somewhat feverish pace he had in such moments, took his black cloak from the coat rack, put it on, and went out.

Ada followed behind him and signalled with her hand for me to come with her. She didn't seem frightened. I had the impression that she was mostly calling me so that I too wouldn't miss something worth seeing.

Outside, the air's purity had turned the sky clear; the moon, a thin crescent, was slanted and low, and the stars close enough to touch, the moon no brighter in comparison.

We felt ourselves undressed, almost as if we had entered into a different space—beyond the earth—where the tepid warmth of our bodies had been sucked out instantaneously by the cold; and at the same time, we were seized, nullified, by the enormous, crushing beauty of the night. In it, Paolo was walking as if on his way to an appointment.

When he reached the stream—Ada choked back a small cry, but he had already stopped—he bent down, stretched out a hand towards the dark water reflecting in little waves the light of the stars, wetted his fingers and wiped them against his forehead.

He turned around, retraced his steps. He hung up his cloak, sat back down at the table and, while Ada gave a reassuring look to the Major and his wife, grabbed his spoon to start eating again.

"It's cold," he said. In their surprise, in their apprehension, none of them had thought to keep his soup warm.

Nani broke out laughing; she laughed so heartily, and for so long, that the other children started laughing too; and everything livened up again, after freezing in dismay, like a *tableau vivant* that had truly come to life.

What's more, we—Ada and I—hadn't really experienced fear, but an emotion just as intense and deep: we were left with an impression of something mysterious, not of illness.

It was still something born of his affliction, but it seemed in some way freed—become, in a manner that escaped us, unclouded and meaningful.

XLIII

I liked the maids at Tetto Murato. It also happened to be true that I liked everything at Tetto Murato; but I liked the maids more than the Fantonis, for instance. I lived in the centre of Tetto Murato, so to speak, and everything that fell on the margins of that world became blurred to me, clouded by fog. The Fantonis, although they lived within the actual walls of Tetto Murato, ended up in fact falling into that neutral and insignificant region; as did the cousins, they too at the edges of that world and its days.

(Only Stefano lived in the very heart of that most secret of worlds despite being far away, and was always present in it.) The maids weren't, therefore, at the margins for me—nor were the children—even if I exchanged very few words with them, an occasional nod or greeting. And so I wasn't surprised when Bruna called me. I liked Bruna more, with her pale and somewhat enigmatic face, than simple-hearted Domenica. They had heard a hubbub going on outside, with people running and shouting, all of which was out of the ordinary at Tetto Murato; and Bruna had called me, not looking pale as usual, but rosy-cheeked and out of breath.

"Come—come and see. The men just got here. Now they're going to pull out the baby calf."

They had found out that the commotion was for a cow who was having a difficult birth. But why had Bruna thought of me, I wondered? I must have seemed like a young girl to her, even though I was married, because I didn't have children, and she must have supposed that this novelty would be for me, as it was for her, exciting.

Soon we were running across the frozen farmyards, along paths covered in hardened and filthy snow, farmyards I had never crossed and that seemed big to me, encircled by the low, black houses.

I wasn't the least bit sure the whole thing appealed to me, and I was even embarrassed about having immediately caved to her invitation. When I'd told Paolo, I could see from his eyes that he was poking fun at me: going out of one's way to see something was exactly the kind of thing he would never do.

The cattle barn was strangely big, and light flooded in through a window; I was surprised because I'd known the barns in those parts to be small and dark. It looked like a regular room, and yet, sure enough, there was the feeding trough, the hay.

The animal was tied up with ropes to keep her still, her back hoofs pulled apart so that she looked as if she might split in two, her wild eyes dilated in terror.

The small crowd of breathless women and children kept to the side, caught between excitement and horror.

Only the men acted: one poured a bucket of water onto the cow's muzzle, two were pulling, trying to free the calf.

There was an obscure, prehistoric grandeur to all of it.

When we walked back outside, Bruna said, "I felt like I was going to be sick in there."

While crossing the farmyards, no longer in a hurry, but at a slow pace, I saw a greenish swath opening up above us, revealing infinite spaces beyond the opaque winter sky; an inkling—light as a feather—whipped through me in the cold air, a sweet premonition of the end of winter. But then, such sweetness—a first hint of sweetness—was also distress: my fear that with the passing of time I would have to face something of my own; that, essentially, I would have to suffer.

In the bedroom, I evaded Paolo's ironic looks. Instead I asked Ada something I already knew.

"Was Paolo there with you when Alessandra was born?"

I knew that Paolo had been there by her side, and knew that when he found her at the hospital, even though she had already started to feel the first pains, she was by a stranger's bedside, helping her to be brave. But what I wanted to know now was something else entirely. However, Ada only distractedly replied that, yes, Paolo had been with her.

Paolo didn't say anything then and there. Later, when we were alone, and the topic had already been dropped for some time, he brought it up again. He said:

"Having a child is also what you saw."

XLIV

Ada went on her bicycle to the village at the foot of the hills—the icy, ploughed roads were easy enough to ride on—and came back looking sullen, agitated.

The men had come down from the mountains to the valley, and it was impossible to really say who had control over the village. You could just as easily run into one side patrolling its streets as the other.

"If they've come down, it's because they know it won't be long now," people were saying in the shop. Ada wanted to hurry and bring us the news; but when she exited onto the small piazza, she saw two men standing right in the middle, facing each other.

A silence, which was not the village's usual silence, had settled, while a vast emptiness surrounded them: the locals peeked out, partially hidden, from their doorways.

Ada stood still too, her hands already gripping the handle-bars.

The man with his back to her seemed to be the younger of the two. He wasn't tall, but nimble, broad-shouldered: he was carrying a Sten gun and wearing a new windproof jacket.

The other man, whose face Ada could see, was tall, no longer young; he was holding a little boy's hand, and his face was horribly, shamefully pale.

The young man must have just insulted him: he was looking down at the ground in silence. Ada saw the young man raise his hand and hit him right across the face, once, then a second time. It all happened very quickly. The young man walked off confidently. The older man didn't react, and instead turned slowly; and, until he was gone, no one moved or so much as breathed.

Ada, who always wanted to see the true side of things, herself included, said that she didn't know how to fully explain why she had felt so awful.

The man who had been hit must have been, as the villagers said, a spy, and in such circumstances a slap from an armed man was like a caress: had it been, Ada wondered, the fact that the boy had been there too, maybe his son?

Ada came to the conclusion that violence, even when just, was frightening, and that maybe justice, for that reason, was all the more commendable.

XLV

It's true that when the end already seems near, there is always still a stretch of time left. A time of patience, for many; and, for others, perhaps a "time to repent"?

And so there were still raids and roundups in the valleys, and the season gave way once more to snow.

At Tetto Murato, Paolo was again held in the grip of recurring pain. But it was no longer as before. Which is to say that Ada and I were no longer struck by it as we had once been, even if Paolo, visibly, wasn't suffering any less. By now we had our sights set on a renewal which we thought of as total, almost as if we could actually know that Paolo, too, would soon be freed.

When leaving Tetto Murato to head towards the road, I often found the Major busying himself in front of the house or in the entrance: he would be adjusting the springs and the screws of a little iron bed for the children, or trying to straighten the end of a bent nail by hitting it with a hammer.

He would jump to his feet to greet me, and apologize: "Times like these, you have to do a bit of everything." But he never appeared embarrassed or upset to me. Ada, however, told me that one day she had gone down to the kitchen and caught him off guard in front of the cupboard, or rather standing on top of a footstool, wearing an apron and rolling out the pasta dough with a rolling pin. She stood there tongue-tied for a second (and she must have laughed, with her eyes). He then begged her tactfully, though, Ada noted, somewhat firmly, too: "You have to promise me, Signora Ada, that when we see each other again—afterwards—you'll forget that you saw me like this."

Naturally, Ada had promised, but in that same instant she had felt sure, "dead sure", in fact, that she would never be able to see him, anywhere, in any circumstances, without picturing him as she saw him now, with pushed-up sleeves and an apron, standing on a stool and rolling out pasta.

Then there was another story about the Fantonis. It was, in a sense, the pinnacle of their famous perfectionism: an excess of prudence, which reached the realm of fantasy.

What had happened was this: the Major had dug a trench behind the house and had stocked it with wicker-wrapped bottles full of water, which he refilled every so often, "in case of an attack".

Instead, what did come to pass was the very thing Signora Sibilla had foretold. Bruna was arrested, in the village.

The Fantonis, according to Ada, took it well: they proved to be less afraid when confronted with real danger than with the imaginary kind.

Bruna wasn't taken into town, but held in the village, in the school that had been converted to a prison. The Fantonis sent her food and clothes, and waited, calmly enough, to see what happened. It didn't occur to them that it could come to light through their interrogations that someone like Paolo was hiding at Tetto Murato.

Ada, for this reason, harboured a silent, almost subterranean fear. She managed to hide it from Paolo, since in those days she was giving him—or was pretending to give him—the cold shoulder.

She sulked, in her light way, when she was around him, slightly stiffening or hesitating, or acting in sudden haste; because she suspected—and it wasn't that she was suspicious of Paolo, really, but of his insidious, tortuous malady—suspected that something in him wanted, truly "wanted" to appear, to disappear, reappear. Ada had even obtained a considerable victory over *it* (the demon was genderless in Ada's mind) through her own cleverness. She had—with naïve yet logical cleverness—injected water instead of the usual medicine, and his agony had subsided all the same.

I thought it wasn't surprising that the trick had worked and that it had obtained an identical result, but I was surprised by Ada. I looked at her with the special kind of admiration she inspired in me at certain times. That she would not only do, dare, but dare this: a gag, a joke concerning the most serious, the most tragic thing in her life.

If the demon was stupid, Paolo wasn't. The second time—impossible to say what had made him suspicious—Paolo wanted to see the vial.

XLVI

I was nearing Tetto Murato after taking the long road; I had run the risk of going on my bicycle because they weren't keeping as close an eye on the roads now, rarely asking if you had authorization. The way was hard, because the snow had melted, flooding the road, and a crust of ice, though fragile, had formed once again on its surface, so that you moved forward as in a pool full of glass shards.

Half on my bicycle—when I could get the wheels to turn—half carrying it in my arms just above the ground, I was resolutely pushing my way through this obstacle course when I suddenly found the road blocked by a tall military truck, completely stuck in the sludge.

On it, looking strangely absent-minded, German soldiers sat close together in rows. Below, two or three were busying themselves around the wheels.

There was no way for me to pass. In my moment of hesitation, as I wondered if I could make an about-turn, one of those giants picked up my bicycle, which looked like a twig, and carried it to the other side, behind the bulky mass of the truck.

My own fear of the Germans ended in that moment. It wasn't that they appeared any less frightening because they were courteous—rather, it was because they seemed to me not only already lost, but even, already saved.

There was cause for celebration at Tetto Murato because Bruna had returned. No one had seen those Germans of mine, and my adventure didn't leave much of an impression on anyone.

XLVII

The seasons suddenly changed, and the midday sun regained a calm autumnal indolence.

Upon arriving, I would see Paolo sitting in the sun on the disjointed planks of a wooden balcony, and I'd scurry up a steep stepladder to join him.

From up there we could take in the snow melting all around us.

The February sun burned brighter than it had in the autumn, and yet—maybe because Paolo was there, just as he had been then—it truly felt to me like a return, a happy loop in time.

In the sleepiness of that hour, and in the security that Paolo's presence gave me, I paid no attention to my premonitions about the future.

When Paolo wasn't in his spot, and therefore had likely stayed in bed, I wouldn't become afraid, but would weigh our present happiness, telling myself that we had accepted his getting better (I didn't dare think: his recovery) without feeling sufficiently grateful.

Ada would reassure me. "He's only being lazy."

★

I was sitting where I always did, only a bit closer to the foot of the bed, because Ada was there too, seated next to Paolo and focused on mending a piece of clothing. Paolo was propped up, leaning against the headboard. The room was full of light, the clear afternoon sun.

I was in a bit of a daze, incredibly sleepy. Coming there under the already hot sun had worn me out; I had walked carrying my coat, which was heavy and had made me sweat. Like wine, the sun had dulled my senses, and my head was throbbing.

I said, "I'm just going to rest here for a second." I laid my bent arm on the bed and fell asleep.

But it wasn't a deep sleep, because soon I heard Paolo and Ada having a conversation. Since they were talking about me, right away I was completely—no, painfully awake. I didn't move, I almost didn't dare breathe.

"She's tired," they said. I heard their voices as extremely close, subdued but clear; I knew that they were there, that I could touch them, and yet it was as if they were very far away. Even more, it was as if I myself were far away while I listened; as if all of it were taking place elsewhere, in a dream, and, just like in a dream, everything I was hearing was in some way dictated by me.

Paolo's voice had never sounded so gentle, and Ada seemed to be playing a game, exactly as she always did when speaking very seriously, and as one would've had to imagine her when dreaming of her.

"She said that she doesn't want to stay over tonight. You tell her too."

"We shouldn't insist. Don't forget that she has her cousins. She has to live with them."

"Yes, yes. We shouldn't make things hard for her."

"Remember that Signora Sibilla is right around here, and she's a friend of theirs."

"Oh, I trust Sibilla."

"Okay—but they could say something."

"The Fantonis? No, no way."

"I wouldn't be so sure. Actually, it's a fact that they talk about it. She often stays the night, too. And don't think they don't also know about the bed."

"Yes, maybe," Ada sighed. (I "saw" her face, when she said no, when she said yes.)

There was a silence. Then Paolo said:

"You know, she might be a little in love with me. You see how far she comes every day…"

"Oh, yes. I think so too."

Paolo didn't speak.

"It's so natural, really. It couldn't not happen. She's just like you."

"And I think I'm a little in love with her."

"I thought so. Do you remember when you'd go with her for part of her walk back in the evening? I'd see you from afar. I'd think that you two were good together."

Another silence. Then Ada started speaking again.

"But you tire her out. You make her think too much with your discussions. You keep her awake all night."

"We talk. Sometimes she falls asleep talking."

Ada didn't speak. Then said:

"Poor Giulia. We'll never love her enough."

They didn't say more. Still, I didn't dare move; I feared that in revealing that I was not asleep, I would seem too awake. Finally, I began to lift my head. Ada asked me, "Did you manage to rest a little?"—the same words and the same tone with which she often questioned Paolo after his brief spurts of sleep.

"Yes. But I have to go."

"Do what you like," Ada said. It was a normal thing for her to say, but I gave a start, because it was confirmation of what I had heard, proof that I hadn't been dreaming.

After, I tried to overcome the kind of violence I had experienced. I told myself that it was not a beginning, but an end, even if it was in some sense an infinite end. I told myself too that if Paolo had spoken in that way with her, it meant that "in the beginning" was Ada, that she came first. (And, for that matter, if it had been up to me, would I have wanted it any other way?)

I clung ever more tightly to Ada; I drew strength from the thought of her: almost as if, in some way, I could share in her mysterious assuredness.

XLVIII

Stefano came for Easter, making one of his adventurous journeys, in a German truck between barrels of gasoline. He was the one to suggest we go to Tetto Murato. We walked there with the road soft from the thawed snow, the sun in our eyes. I darted glances at Stefano as he spoke; I was happy that he was seeing my road in this way, too, during the waning of winter.

Stefano placed a handful of red berries in my palm, which he had grabbed from the bushes. So, he still could—in times such as these in which he was rapidly maturing—find our old games again.

While I sucked on the sweet-bitter berries, cooked by the freezing cold of the long winter, I started to skip, hanging on to Stefano's arm: I felt irresponsible and happy. Stefano's being at Tetto Murato was for me like the world had regained—temporarily—its unity.

At Tetto Murato, we immediately, spontaneously divided up tasks. Stefano stayed in the kitchen with Ada, while she made tea. I went upstairs to Paolo.

He was, as she said, oppressed, and he greeted me with only a feeble smile. I moved the chair next to the bed and curled up in my usual position.

Ada and Stefano came in, she holding the basket tray, he opening the door to let her through and bending towards her while she told him a story.

Paolo shook himself back to life, refused the dreadful green tea, but was affectionate, forcing himself to talk; it seemed to me that he was looking at Stefano with a kind of admiration and almost astonishment (a little like he was seeing him for the first time).

There was another moment, not long before we had to leave, in which we had split into groups. I was in my spot next to the bed: Paolo was silent, while Ada and Stefano were talking to each other.

They were standing, one in front of the other, by the western window, which let in the warm light of the sunset.

I had followed Paolo's gaze and turned to look at them.

Stefano, who had his back to me, spoke slightly bent towards Ada, and I could glimpse her uplifted face, her big eyes which were focused yet vague, mysterious.

I turned back to Paolo: he was still looking at them, now with that knowing smile of his.

"You see how they get along. Maybe they don't even know how much they were made to understand each other."

(Maybe Paolo said, "they, too"—I couldn't say for sure, and in the end it was the same thing.)

My way of seeing the truth within myself was not rapid and

resolute as Ada's. But I too knew how to freeze before that to which I could not give a name.

No doubt, Paolo meant to say once again, as he had expressly said other times before: They are better than us.

I, who already instinctively considered Stefano and Ada superior, unreachable, not only relative to myself but to Paolo, too, I had for a second the somewhat dizzying impression that our way of being was if not suggested, then almost guided, allowed by them.

XLIX

What followed were the most peaceful days. Ada and I were nearly jubilant; Paolo, on the other hand, impatient about doing nothing. He was translating a classic too, when he felt up to it; but that wasn't what he was after at this point. He was impatient, but not uneasy, because he was no longer ill.

They were just a few days, really, but they constituted a whole period of time, full to the brim.

They were peaceful days, and yet the delicate April sky seemed as though it couldn't contain the compact, constant rumbling of airplanes.

There was, in us and in that time of year, a stillness, a kind of ripening, in the sense that something had become stable, tranquil.

It was a day like the others, full of sunlight, of the clucking of chickens, of the sounds of children playing.

Paolo left it up to Ada to say it. Ada announced, calmly, "Paolo has decided to go to Turin." "When?" (I knew that the answer could even be: tomorrow.) "The day after tomorrow."

I was given a few tasks: find someone in town who could host Paolo the night before he left for Turin, and similar things. I would be the one to go with Paolo to town; Domenica would bring the suitcase on the bicycle.

We went at a brisk pace, because Paolo didn't like to walk slowly; I snuck glances at him to see if he was showing signs of exhaustion. He was panting a bit, and halfway there he suggested we sit on the ground by the side of the road.

Only then did I look around me. The countryside and the sky seemed restrained, suspended in a placid and solemn sadness.

Lowering my eyes, I saw, right there at our feet, close to our hands which were resting on the short grass scattered with dried blades, violets: little shaggy tufts of them.

We spoke little and only about practical matters for the moment at hand. To avoid the checkpoint at the entrance to the main bridge, we turned off the road onto a path that went meandering towards a footbridge over the river, one that wasn't surveilled. Sure enough, no one stopped us.

When we were close enough to see the house which belonged to a friend, we stopped in the empty street and said goodbye to each other. We shook hands: "Bye, Giulia." "Bye, Paolo." (More or less like children parting ways at the end of a holiday.) But then he added, "Don't worry."

L

When the town was liberated, again the cousins had on the same face from the 25th of July, like "nothing had happened". I was always out of the house: the old town of penetrating silences, now full of young life, surprised me to no end.

I expected that at any given moment I might see Paolo. One day, returning to the cousins' house, I found out that he had come to see me, but that he had left right away. I got over that first mishap—in those days it was impossible to feel any disappointment. Ada, who had left Tetto Murato, ran to the house to see me and was so happy she hugged the cousins, too; they were taken aback, stiffening up a little out of surprise, but they smiled at her, and they seemed blissfully happy about it to me.

I saw Paolo again among many other people: he had a slightly tired and abstracted air about him, which I had already noticed on the 25th of July (and which had disappointed me then, because I had expected more joy). He smiled at me with his eyes, and I was content with that feeling of complicity which isolated us, and which was still Tetto Murato.

Then one day I left suddenly because I'd been offered a means to reach Stefano. I said goodbye to Ada and Paolo lightheartedly, almost festively, sure that I would see them again soon (without asking myself when). Everything was possible, the future open; I had no fear whatsoever.

When the time came to say goodbye to the cousins, however, I was struck with uncertainty. I wasn't going to see them again, I thought. I discovered—like someone who has always seen, for example, a house, considering it average, devoid of any mystery, and then one day glimpses in it the possibility of a secret, of a story—discovered that there was something in them that I hadn't known, that I hadn't had time to come to know. I felt a kind of remorse, and asked them—generically—for their forgiveness.

They replied, somewhat moved, that there was no need for that, and the harshest thing they said was that all faults are reciprocal and, between people who love each other, involuntary.

L I

In Milan I went up many flights of stairs in a building that reminded me of the one where I had gone to look for Paolo in Turin.

I knocked; Stefano appeared hesitant too, caught in a daydream, as though only my image had appeared before him and not actually me. He turned pale when I approached him.

Stefano, as well, prepared something to eat with his hands. He cut up an onion and cooked it with rice, in the only pot. We ate using the only two pieces of silverware, one with broken prongs, the other with a broken handle. (I had learned to be grateful for even the little that was still good in things.)

The bedframe was made of iron like the one at the cousins' house, and it wasn't very big either. The weather was of spring-summer, and the two of us lay on that bed like on a tropical island besieged by crocodiles: around us, black roaches scurried quickly on the floor.

Stefano was full of love for that liberated city which, lifted out of its nightmares, was young in its popular dances in the evenings, in courtyards just recently swept clean of debris and rubble and now cheerfully draped with red flags.

Stefano was—and in this he truly resembled Ada—intent on the present and full of love for it, but he also had his sights set hopefully on tomorrow.

When the two of us talked, I too managed to believe that we could bring Paolo and Ada with us, and I'd dream up plans for a life in which we weren't pulled apart. But when I was alone, I felt Tetto Murato as something lost.

I rebelled against this feeling; I wanted for Tetto Murato to continue. I was sure that it could go on elsewhere, that it was still possible for it to exist on this earth, as it had before.

I would close my eyes, and the game was to wait for something to show itself to me.

It would be the western window, the calm light of the sunset entering the room, and with it, a long silence, broken in the end by some exclamation of Ada's, or by Nani's shy knocking at the door. Or, from the window on the stairs, the light of the stars over the countryside, in the freezing night air. Or noises, sounds: the crowing of roosters, distant barking, the clucking of hens; or, close by, the door groaning—deep, slow, familiar. And the smells: the scent of manure or of the chicken coop, in the front hall, in the yards; in the house, the damp smell of mildew, or the dry smell of grain; the aroma, in the kitchen, of smoke and apples.

As is often the case with people who care deeply for one another, we didn't write much: occasional updates, and those too were vague. Paolo's illness was never mentioned, just as one did not speak of past suffering. The only person to bring it up was Stefano, who must have written a special letter once, because Ada alluded to it later, as to something too beautiful to talk about.

Sometimes, when I wasn't thinking of them, but more often right when I was thinking of them, Stefano would say, "Those poor things. Who knows…" I'd laugh at "those poor things", which sounded like an expression from Alessandro Manzoni, but then I'd think back on how Ada used to "feel bad" for Stefano.

Immediately, I'd reply that they weren't—shouldn't be—poor things any more, not now. Stefano would end the conversation with a (non-Manzonian) "I'd eat my hat if…" A sentence that hung there, and left a bad feeling.

LII

Only in late autumn, on the eve of our moving to the capital, did I travel to see Paolo and Ada again.

I wanted my arrival to be unexpected, even if it meant running the risk of not finding them in.

I was not disappointed, naturally, by the way Ada welcomed me. She shouted, held out her arms to greet me. Then she calmed down, and said with abandon, "Oh, Giulia, I have only you." It was one of her old expressions, the kind that made you want to throw yourself into the fire for her.

But there was also a hint of exhaustion, a shadow under Ada's eyes. And the house had a strange look of order-disorder about it. "Are you moving?"

"We're going back to Turin." She said it coolly.

She hadn't mentioned Paolo. I didn't have a lot of time. I asked, "Paolo?" "He's in there," she replied, still coldly. At that point I feared I had guessed, but I didn't want to accept it: "No!" "Yes," she said harshly. "Since when?" "You know how it is. It can stop at any moment."

Meanwhile she took an armful of sheets and headed towards the hallway. "Come. I have to pack the trunks."

I followed her. Ada walked lightly, holding the things high, with her slightly abrupt, dancelike movements. (She was wearing her signature robe.)

From the door to the bedroom, my gaze ran to the unmade bed, to Paolo's side specifically, but it was empty. Ada pointed to the floor. Paolo was there, lying flat and composed, his arms at his sides, his eyes closed. In my mind I ran to him, I bent over his body. Instead I only looked at him.

We went back into the dining room. The paintings had already been taken down: Paolo's mother was no longer there, gone her gaze brimming with sadness.

Nani walked into the room, holding the hand of a small countrywoman—dark, with a gizzard-like neck and a pitch-black gaze. Nani was holding on to her with the same trust and the same detachment with which she used to hold Domenica's hand.

"Domenica?"

"She's with her husband."

We returned to the other room. Paolo, there on the ground, not looking meek, but disdainful, alone. Ada went back to putting things in order. Because Paolo was lying between the dresser and the wardrobe, Ada, instead of going around him, went over him each time she needed to get by: the way she might have hopped over a log or a stream in a field.

She said, "Are you going over to the cousins' house?" "I won't see them. I'm leaving right away." "You're leaving?" She put down what she was holding; she sat down, letting her arms fall to her sides as though a great misfortune had just come to pass.

I felt ashamed for causing her pain. I would have preferred not to have come at all.

"And Paolo? He won't see you?" She ran over to him, bent down to lift his hand, let it fall; his hand made a thud. She looked disappointed, as with a machine that won't start when needed; she wasn't thinking about Paolo's illness at this point, only about the fact that he wouldn't see me.

She straightened back up, letting out a quick sigh. Rapidly she turned to the bed, tidied the blankets, tucked them in: they were Tetto Murato gestures.

Then we hugged each other goodbye, since she didn't have time to go and see me off. She seemed thin, fragile in my arms. "I can't even go with you," she said, and smiled.

Afterword

by Lalla Romano

NOTE, 1985

A young reader told me that after reading *A Silence Shared* (*Tetto Murato*) he was left with clearly imprinted images: the protagonist (or rather, the person who says "I") grabs a fallen apple in a field, a German soldier picks up her bicycle like a twig, and many others.

Truly, *A Silence Shared* is a novel full of images; beyond that, one could say the same thing about my other books, and it would be easy to point to the author's former experience as a painter, thanks to which her imagination, even her memory, are "visual". In any case, the images are rarely a cultural reference, and for the most part are immediate, lived.

What effect do they have on the reader? The young reader I've spoken of found them essential, not ornamental, not added on. It's true that this reader is passionate about photography, and that such an interest is very widespread, one could say vital, in this day and age.

Well, it must have been this *visuality* that was judged fatuous by Paolo Milano, who titled his review of *A Silence Shared* "The Aesthetes of the Resistance". Firstly, it was a mistake for him to place those two terms together; the aestheticism—if there is any—certainly does not concern the Resistance.

But before getting to the historical setting, I'd like to reflect more on the role of images. Commenting on an exhibition of Dutch painters (Vermeer, de Hooch), Giorgio Zampa noted that those paintings "describe, rather than narrate". I recognized myself in this line: I've always known that my talent is not specifically a narrative one. And yet I write novels, which have readers who are not particularly visual, I imagine.

My books are not "of the gaze": the images are a means (a matter of taste), not an end. They may not lend themselves to representing external conflicts or historical adventures and privilege a certain immobility, even if they do enter into the flow of time, into the unfolding of the story as it's marked by passing days and seasons. It's pretty extraordinary that from this seemingly drawn-out rhythm emerges a tension, an almost urgent sense of waiting, one that is evidently interior and a little mysterious.

A definition that annoyed me back then was that of the "intimist novel". I didn't take it in its more innocuous, classifi-catory sense—to me it seemed as though it were alluding to a kind of indulgent sentimentalism.

Carlo Salinari judged the book "mature" (in terms of its form, I think), but my having confined the Resistance to the background was unforgivable for him. I was indignant, finding this need for a commemorative scope rhetorical. The historical circumstances were not at all indifferent to the rest of the novel: on the contrary, the possibility of intimacy was offered precisely by that life on the margins, in a forced suspension which entailed concentration and an openness to contemplation, to the discovery of pure, poor beauty; and which fostered, most of all, emotions that were intense yet unspoken, secret.

Henry James—undoubtedly a great intimist—maintains that "the subject is everything". What is the subject of *A Silence Shared*? I remember how embarrassed I felt, upon receiving the Premio Pavese, when a journalist questioned me about "the plot". I gauged all of the awkwardness, the crudeness, of any potential answer I might formulate.

On the back cover of the second edition (1971), an editorial note suggested: "Two young couples, the prison of a long winter: the discovery, through a subtle plot of elective affinities, of the gift of life." The "gift of life" was a variation on Montale's "intellectual love of life", taken from the memorable piece he wrote on *A Silence Shared*; the same goes for the affinities, which were an "underlying theme" revealing other "possible destinies", according, once again, to Montale.

In reality, those themes were already present for me when I was writing, and in reference specifically to two great works: to the book by Goethe, obviously, for "the affinities", and, for "the winter", to *The Magic Mountain*. However, I didn't see them as models, but as obstacles to get around, temptations to avoid. Not only out of modesty.

So, *The Magic Mountain* contained the winter, the snow, as a metaphysical backdrop; but it was most of all a historical-essayistic novel—think of those famous long conversations. In *A Silence Shared* the conversations, frequent and endless, are left unsaid for the reader, and not because I wouldn't have known how to write them. It was a wise decision to have them substituted with brief lines, significant only of the characters' single temperaments and natures. Could its other theme, illness—also present and important in *A Silence Shared*—perhaps be attributed to some symbolic significance? Not necessarily: it's a human condition inherent to the story and to its particular emotional intensity.

The Goethean theme—like those connected to Mann—presented itself to me when I was writing, not before. The book, therefore, isn't born of other books, even if little by little it recalls them, and this evocation itself became a problem, a temptation.

What, then, was the idea (as James called it) at the heart of the book? Maybe the one hinted at in the epigraph: "The only true silence is a silence shared." Solitary silence is mute because it is, in fact, solitude, and soliloquy can become a confession, but not a novel. "Shared" implies the other, which can be, as is the case here, a community.

The striking relevance of that line of Pavese's (taken from *Dialogues with Leucò*) also illuminated for me the meaning of the book: a book which, for that matter, has nothing Pavese-like about it. The small community in *A Silence Shared* was segregated—secret—because it had to stay hidden; but there was a more profound secrecy, too, which brought with it limitations, suffering, though never hypocrisy: because it was natural, necessary. It derived from the "contradictions and ambiguities" of life, and from its "inexplicable dignity" (Montale once more).

And the final conclusion-revelation, the one that Montale called "the right choice," consequently revealed itself. It was the truth of that story, which developed and came to light all on its own.